Lou-lan
and
Other Stories

Yasushi Inoue

Translated by

James T. Araki

Edward Seidensticker

KODANSHA INTERNATIONAL
Tokyo • New York • London

UNESCO COLLECTION OF REPRESENTATIVE WORKS:
JAPANESE SERIES

This book has been accepted as part of the Japanese Series of the
Translations Collection of the United Nations Educational, Scientific and Cultural Organization (UNESCO).

"Lou-lan" and "The Rhododendrons" originally appeared in the
Japan Quarterly, the latter under the title "The Azaleas of Hira."

Distributed in the United States by Kodansha America, Inc., 114
Fifth Avenue, New York, N.Y. 10011, and in the United Kingdom
and continental Europe by Kodansha Europe Ltd., Gillingham
House, 38-44 Gillingham Street, London SW1V 1HU.
Published by Kodansha International Ltd., 17-14 Otowa 1-chome,
Bunkyo-ku, Tokyo 112, and Kodansha America, Inc. Copyright ©
1979 by Kodansha International Ltd. All rights reserved. Printed
in Japan.

LCC 79-66239
ISBN 0-87011-472-7
ISBN 4-7700-0960-7 (in Japan)

First edition, 1979
First paperback edition, 1981
91 92 93 10 9 8 7 6

CONTENTS

Note: Personal names follow the order of the Japanese, that is, with the family name first.

Lou-lan

Translated by
Edward Seidensticker

1

Long ago, on the western frontiers of China, there was a small country called Lou-lan. In about 120 or 130 B.C. the first notice was taken of Lou-lan, and in 77 B.C. it disappeared. Lou-lan thus had its place in history for a total of about fifty years.

Lou-lan was introduced to the Chinese by the famous adventurer Chang Ch'ien, who had been despatched to the northwest by the Han Emperor Wu Ti and who, for his achievements, was honored with the title "Lord of the Wide Vision." Today most of the Western Marches of China are included in Sinkiang Province. Two thousand years ago, however, they were a desert to the northwest of China, an alien land, the dwelling place of Mongols and Tartars. Only much later, with the opening of the caravan route known as the Silk Road, did the Western Marches become a commercial and cultural passageway.

Until the time of Wu Ti, no one had been so intrepid as to set foot in this wilderness. No one knew how far the desert went, or what sort of people lived there, or what countries it contained.

It was not from curiosity about unknown lands or from an explorer's zeal that Wu Ti despatched Chang Ch'ien to the northwest. It was to form an alliance with the Tocharians, a powerful people beyond the unknown desert, and, with them,

7

to beat back the Hsiung-nu, who were a strong and persistent threat to Han China. For more than fifty years, since the reign of Kao Tsu, the Han had been sending princesses in marriage to the Hsiung-nu. They had also sent tribute and permitted trade. The depredations of the Hsiung-nu continued nonetheless.

Each successive emperor had his troubles with them. The Hsiung-nu were a nomadic people who ranged over a wide area to the north of the Han, from Siberia into Central Asia. By nature violent and warlike, they would descend upon Chinese outposts whenever they saw their chance. China enjoyed years without famine or natural disasters, but no year went by without another raid by the Hsiung-nu. The Chinese had thrown all their men and all their horses into the fight. When Wu Ti first campaigned against them, his troops took a Tartar captive, who had this to say: "The Hsiung-nu once killed a king of the Tocharians. They use his skull as a wine cup. The Tocharians therefore hate the Hsiung-nu, but can do nothing by way of revenge because they are without allies." Wu Ti hit upon the idea of sending an emissary to the Tocharians and forming a common front against the Hsiung-nu. He asked for volunteers, and Chang Ch'ien agreed to go. Setting out in 139 B.C. with more than a hundred men who had been slaves of the Hsiung-nu, Chang entered the land of the Mongols and Tartars. He returned thirteen years later, and of the men who had set out with him only a single man accompanied him back. He had spent more than ten years as a prisoner of the Hsiung-nu. Making his escape, he had pushed on across the desert and reached the land of the Tocharians. On the way back he was again captured by the Hsiung-nu, but, taking advantage of civil strife, he escaped and finally reached home.

In 124 B.C. he arrived at Ch'ang-an, the Han capital, and told Wu Ti of the lands, the peoples, and the products of the Western Marches.

Thus Lou-lan first appeared in Chinese history, along with the other small countries in that desert belt: Charchan, Khotan, Yarkand, Karashahr, Kashgar, Kucha, Bugur, and the rest. The *Han Chronicle of the Western Marches* describes the area thus: there were originally thirty-six nations within it, but, through later divisions, the number at times came to more than fifty, all to the west of the Hsiung-nu and south of the Wu-sun. To the north and south lay the great T'ien-shan and K'un-lun ranges respectively, and through the center flowed the Tarim River. More than six thousand *li* from east to west and more than a thousand *li* from north to south, the Marches joined China on the east at the Jade Gate and the Yang Barrier, and on the west were closed off by the Pamir Plateau.

In brief, the Western Marches were what is today known as the Tarim Basin, surrounded on three sides by the T'ien-shan, the K'un-lun, and the Pamir Plateau. The Takla Makan Desert occupies the center. In the oases on the fringes were small city-states, each with its own speech, customs, and color of skin. Although they had been in communication with China before the reign of Wu Ti, it had been of a private nature. Wu Ti was the first to open state-to-state relations.

As one leaves the Jade Gate and the Yang Barrier, one enters a desert belt. Beyond is a lake, Lop Nor, also known to the Chinese as "the briny marsh." Many times the size of the present Lop Nor, it was in Wu Ti's day a vast, shallow, heavily salted lake that might better have been described as a sea. It lay some three hundred *li* beyond the Jade Gate and the Yang Barrier, and into it flowed the Tarim, the great river of the Takla Makan Desert.

The nearest of the small countries to China, Lou-lan lay on the northwest shore. At Lou-lan the road from Han China divided, one branch veering south along the north slope of the K'un-lun range, the other north along the southern slope of T'ien-shan. The southern road passed Charchan, Khotan, Yarkand and Bugur, and eventually led to the Tocharians. The northern road passed Turfan, Karashahr, Kashgar, and Kucha on the way to the Wu-sun and Fergana. Whether going to the north or the south, the traveler from Han through the Western Marches had to pass Lou-lan.

The *Han Chronicle of the Western Marches* says of Charkhlik, the successor to Lou-lan: "It has 1,570 households, 14,100 people, and 2,912 stalwart warriors." From this we may imagine the size of Lou-lan itself. There was a country of about fourteen or fifteen thousand people, then, on the northwest shore of Lop Nor. They were an Aryan race of Iranian stock, dark, with deep-set eyes, high noses, and, in general, boldly incised features. They lived by farming and herding, and by taking salt and fish from the lake.

Although they were introduced to history by Chang Ch'ien, they must have been living on this shore for some hundreds of years already. Until they struck up relations with the Han, they were in constant danger from the Hsiung-nu, and suffered terribly from their attacks. Lou-lan managed nonetheless to survive, a tiny nation of fourteen or fifteen thousand people on the beautiful shore of Lop Nor. It was too small to resist the Hsiung-nu, but man for man its warriors were good fighters. They were skilled horsemen, and their special tactics with war chariots were the bane of their neighbors.

Wu Ti sent Chang Ch'ien abroad in an attempt to form a common front against the Hsiung-nu. He received an equivocal answer from the Tocharians, however, rather than the news he had hoped to have from his ambassador. He nonetheless gained from Chang's report one thing that was unexpected and important: an awareness of the small countries in the Western Marches.

Strategically, they were of great value against the Hsiung-nu. With them under his control, Wu Ti could threaten the Hsiung-nu flank. He could also use their armies. The little countries of the desert basin moreover produced numbers of rare and valuable products. They had jade, of course, and amber. They had gold and silver and copper. They had salt and spices and wine. Horses, water buffaloes, elephants, peacocks, rhinoceroses, lions. They had fruits in plenty, and the five cereals. Through trade with them the finances of the Han state, badly drained in the struggle with the Hsiung-nu, could be replenished. Especially attractive to Wu Ti, who was suffering from a shortage of horses, were the fine steeds of Fergana.

Wu Ti also learned the names of great countries beyond the Western Marches. He did not know exactly where Sogdiana and Parthia and India were, but he did know that they were exceedingly large countries and that their lands were rich. India especially interested him—a hot country some thousands of *li* to the south and east of Bactria. He was most impressed to learn that it was possible to reach India without fear of the Hsiung-nu, and that its people wished to trade.

In 122 B.C. Wu Ti again ordered Chang Ch'ien to the Western Marches. The mission this time was to reach India and ask that communications be opened. His way blocked by the southwestern barbarians, however, Chang was forced to turn back.

The next year he departed on a third trip. The Han armies had attacked the Hsiung-nu and taken the land around Tunhuang, until then held by the nomads. Not wishing to lose the opportunity which control of the road to the Western Marches offered, Wu Ti for the first time sent Chang Ch'ien to propose friendly commerce with the countries of the region. The year was 121 B.C.

꧁

The people of Lou-lan first saw Han troops on the occasion of Chang Ch'ien's third expedition to the Western Marches. Having had warning of a Han attack, the little citadel on the shore of Lop Nor was in a state of consternation. Some thousands of horses and camels, usually left to graze outside, had been brought within the walls, the seven gates were tightly barricaded, and armed warriors had been posted at every vantage point around the wall.

The waters of Lop Nor stretched quietly away like a blue cloth. The lake, thick with brine, became turbulent at the lightest wind, so that its calmness that day filled the people of Lou-lan with a deep uneasiness. Close to the shore the waters were greenish, and in the distance they approached indigo. Along the north shore of the lake a forest stretched away as far as one could see. Mostly it was a forest of poplar, but here and there it was broken by patches of tamarisk and other shrubs to form a checkered pattern. To the south, the shore was choked with reeds and rushes. Numerous streams flowed into the lake, but one saw them only upon reaching the banks, so overgrown were they.

There were also streams running through the walled town itself. Except for the forest to the north of the lake, the land was for league upon league a network of streams, between which lay cultivated land. Some were artificial, but many were dry beds into which the water of the Tarim, about a *li* from the town, had been diverted. To describe it precisely, then, Lou-lan, although it lay in a desert belt, was a fortified town on the fertile delta of the Tarim River, by the shores of Lop Nor.

A road ran along the north bank of the Tarim. For the most part the river was concealed by trees and shrubbery, but there was one stretch where it showed itself, a clear blue. Some years before, it had changed its course, and there alone no trees hid it from the sky. The road too was stripped of covering along this one stretch.

The men on the walls of Lou-lan had for some time been watching a long line of men and animals, small as grains of wheat, on that stretch of road. It took rather a long time for one of the tiny figures to emerge from the forest and disappear into the forest again. Three of the men on the wall had been selected for their ability to see into the distance. They would count off the numbers of the men and beasts in the column, and others would relay the count in loud voices to the foot of the wall, whence it would in turn be passed on to the outer defenses.

A wasted old man of seventy-eight had the keenest vision in the country. His remarkably small eyes took the count of three hundred men, about twice that number of horses, and more than ten thousand sheep and cattle. He saw, moreover, that about half the horses were heavily loaded. His tense face relaxed, for it was evident that the Han force had not come to make war.

The stir within the walls was now of a different nature. Yet though they knew that they did not face immediate attack the men of Lou-lan were cautious. It was not till two days later that stations were abandoned, supplies and treasures were taken out of cellars, and horses and camels were once more turned out to graze. For some days afterwards the men of Lou-lan asked one another why this great Han force had headed into the Western Marches without despatching an emissary to their city. Six months later their king learned that Chang had taken the northern route and established friendly relations with the Wu-sun, the most powerful people to the north of the Takla Makan, and that the Chinese had then broken into smaller missions to Fergana, Sogdiana, the Tocharians, Bactria, Parthia, Khotan, and India. It became clear that they had purposely avoided Lou-lan, which was under the sway of the Hsiung-nu, as well as Turfan, which, like it, lay at the entrance to the Western Marches and was at the mercy of the Hsiung-nu.

Almost every month thereafter, the people of Lou-lan saw Han forces of various sizes heading west and heading east. And not only Han: there were scores of Wu-sun with horses and camels, passing from the Tarim basin to China; and every day, or every few days at the most, there would be small parties from Bactria, heading east, again with horses and camels. Although it was of no concern to the people of Lou-lan, they had before their eyes evidence that relations between the Han and nations to the west were daily growing closer.

Sometimes the people of Lou-lan left their citadel and went off across the wide fields to the Tarim for a close look at the travelers. In all the time since they had come to live by Lop Nor they had never before had such an opportunity.

The men of Lou-lan thought that they would not again see the Hsiung-nu. They had heard that the Han had routed the nomads and they were not beyond believing the rumors. They had been told by travelers that there were Han stations at Chiu-ch'üan and Tun-huang, once Hsiung-nu strongholds, that the Great Wall had been extended to Chiu-ch'üan, that to the west of Tun-huang there were numerous beacon towers and strong points, among them the Jade Gate and the Yang Barrier, and that communication routes between Han China and the Western Marches had been secured.

Thus Lou-lan passed two years free from the ravages of the Hsiung-nu.

The first emissary from the Han came in the autumn of the third year after Lou-lan had sighted Han troops. The purpose of the visit was to hand down a Han order: Lou-lan was to despatch appropriate numbers of men to replenish the food and water of Han expeditions leaving the Jade Gate and the Yang Barrier for the Western Marches. Turfan received the same order.

Thus Lou-lan had to send large numbers of men into the desert day after day. It was not easy, going out loaded with food and water for the Chinese. The men of Lou-lan had long suffered under the Hsiung-nu, but the new order, with the military power of China behind it, was no easier to bear.

About a month after they had been forced to start sending men not into the fields but, heavily loaded, into the desert, the people of Lou-lan awoke to a sound they had long been spared: the neighing of Hsiung-nu ponies. Ten and more Hsiung-nu warriors forced their way through the gates and galloped through the streets, to show the people of Lou-lan that the Hsiung-nu were still alive and able. On the spears of the young warriors were freshly taken Chinese heads, dripping with blood and blue in the moonlight.

The next day the young men of Lou-lan who went into the desert killed three Chinese travelers, and in the evening they brought their booty back to the city. They were received with jubilation. If Lou-lan was to be a subject nation in any case, its people thought that they would choose the Hsiung-nu, with whom their relations had been close, over the unknown Chinese.

Chinese travelers were killed in the desert again the next day. The men of Lou-lan did not go again into the desert to serve the Chinese. Soon Hsiung-nu forces were stationed in both Lou-lan and Turfan. The young men of Lou-lan frequently attacked Chinese parties.

It was early in the winter of 108 B.C. that the Chinese first joined battle in the desert of the Western Marches with the Hsiung-nu, who had once more advanced upon the region of the Jade Gate and the Yang Barrier. A Han general, Chao P'o-nu, at the head of tens of thousands of men, marched to the west and sent the Hsiung-nu flying to the north. Carried on by the impetus of this victory, he turned toward Lop Nor. His purpose was to attack Lou-lan and Turfan.

Lou-lan was surrounded by Han troops before anyone knew what was happening. There was no time to prepare, so swift had the Han advance been. When a Han officer came through the gate at the head of seven hundred men, there was nothing for the people within to do but watch with folded arms. The Han soldiers entered the king's mansion at the center of the city. The king was promptly made captive.

The king of Lou-lan was taken off to Chao P'o-nu's camp

and there forced to swear allegiance to the Han. In the course of the evening he sent his eldest son off as a hostage to the Han court.

Having thus taken Lou-lan, the Han forces marched on to Turfan, and thence to Fergana and the land of the Wu-sun, from which they withdrew the following spring.

The Hsiung-nu, who had been lying in wait, struck when they were gone. The king of Lou-lan was forced to submit to them as he had submitted to the Han, and this time his second son went as a hostage.

Wu Ti had come to use force in his management of the Western Marches. Angered that Fergana had refused to exchange horses for gold and had in fact put the Han ambassador to death, he despatched a punitive expedition. In 103 B.C. Li Kuang-li headed west toward Fergana at the head of six thousand regular cavalrymen and some tens of thousands of irregulars. The states along the way closed themselves in and refused to give him supplies. He did eventually reach Fergana, but only after half his army had died of starvation. He was defeated in battle, and made his way back to the Jade Gate with only a few surviving troops. Angry at this clumsy performance, Wu Ti handed down an order: "They are to be cut down if they try to pass through." The defeated soldiers were thus turned back from the Jade Gate and forced to camp at Tun-huang.

The next year Li Kuang-li again departed from Tun-huang, this time at the head of more than sixty thousand men. He also took a hundred thousand cattle, thirty thousand horses, and tens of thousands of mules and camels. He gave the most careful attention to supplies.

When Li's great army passed Lop Nor, Lou-lan sent out soldiers at the order of the Hsiung-nu to harass the Chinese rear. Their intention was forestalled by the Chinese, however, and Lou-lan was surrounded by soldiers despatched from the Jade Gate. Although they had the help of Hsiung-nu cavalrymen, the men of Lou-lan were unable to hold their city, and their king was once more taken captive by the Chinese.

He reached Ch'ang-an, the Han capital, as reports of victories at Fergana were coming in. The Han expeditionary troops surrounded the Fergana capital, forced its surrender, and took some scores of fine horses and more than three thousand ordinary draft horses.

During his interrogation the king of Lou-lan said: "Mine is a small country between two very large countries, the Han and the Hsiung-nu. It cannot survive without submitting to the two of them. Its people are quite exhausted. If the Han wish to have Lou-lan under their control, there is but one thing they can do: give permission for the whole population of Lou-lan to be resettled on Han soil." Moved by these words, Wu Ti had the king sent back to Lou-lan.

After the conquest of Fergana, the Han built watchtowers at strategic places in the desert between the Jade Gate and Lop Nor, secured the way from China to the Western Marches, and stationed several hundred soldiers in Bugur and along the Tarim River. Whatever its own wishes in the matter, Lou-lan thus fell under the sway of the Han. In 89 B.C. the Han once more attacked Turfan. Lou-lan was ordered to supply troops, and thus to fight the Hsiung-nu who had come to the assistance of Turfan. Lou-lan losses were considerable.

Exhausted by the task of serving both the Han and the Hsiung-nu, the king of Lou-lan fell ill and died. There was no one to succeed him. One of his sons had gone as a hostage to the Han, the other to the Hsiung-nu, and neither had returned. The elder son, the hostage to China, had committed a crime and been put to death. Nothing more had been heard of the second son. A relative of the dead king finally ascended the throne. Hostages were promptly demanded by both countries. His older son, An-kuei, went to the Hsiung-nu, and his second, Wei-t'u-ch'i, to the Han.

Because his finances were strained, because he had lost to

some extent the support of his people, and, finally, because he had grown tired of war, Wu Ti, once so aggressive in ruling the Western Marches, showed signs of waning enthusiasm in his last years. The Hsiung-nu came and went as they would. Most of the states on the roads through the Marches had acknowledged the suzerainty of the Han, but now they began to secede. In keeping with the times, Lou-lan too began to move away from the Han and toward the Hsiung-nu.

The new king, exhausted like his predecessor, died a few years after ascending the throne. The Hsiung-nu returned his elder son, An-kuei, who succeeded to the throne as a young man of twenty-eight. An-kuei was openly friendly toward the Hsiung-nu and hostile toward the Han. He knew how his two predecessors had labored in their double allegiance, and, having long lived among Hsiung-nu, he naturally found them the easier of the two powers to be friendly with.

The policy of the young king soon found expression. Very shortly after his accession a Chinese ambassador invited him to visit the Han court. He declined. And he made his country a Hsiung-nu outpost for obstructing Chinese communications with the countries of the Western Marches. Ambassadors going west from China and tributary missions going east were frequently attacked in the vicinity of Lop Nor.

For some years after An-kuei ascended the throne, Hsiung-nu forces openly moved in and out of Lou-lan. Herds of white Hsiung-nu ponies were always to be seen outside its walls.

The Han Emperor Wu Ti died and was succeeded by Chao Ti.

Among the countries of the Western Marches, Kucha joined Lou-lan in allying itself with the Hsiung-nu. It was exposed to pressure from both the Han and the Hsiung-nu, and its trials had been no different from those of Turfan and Lou-lan. Thus two little countries across the desert from each other threw off their double allegiance, and, though they did not know whether the results would in the end be good or bad, they determined to take their chances with the Hsiung-nu.

The day was inevitable, however, when China would have its revenge. King An-kuei knew this, but he did not think that the revenge would be so swift in coming.

In the autumn of 77 B.C. Lou-lan received a Han emissary, Fu Chieh-tzu. It was his second visit that year. Earlier he had come to reprimand Lou-lan, and An-kuei had sent him back with an apology. There had been no change in An-kuei's policy, however, and the spirited king was somewhat apprehensive at receiving the Han ambassador a second time. Unfortunately, the Hsiung-nu ponies that were usually grazing near the wall had been withdrawn. Helpless, the king of Lou-lan invited the Chinese into the royal mansion.

A banquet was held in the great hall. Fu Chieh-tzu had two attendants with him. The royal family and the ministers of state took their places about the three Chinese.

The banquet was reaching a climax when Fu Chieh-tzu said that there was something he must say to the king alone. The king leaned over to hear what it was. The two Chinese on his right thereupon stabbed him in the back. Amid cries of horror, Fu Chieh-tzu stood up and, glaring at the assembly, bellowed out his message. His face was like that of a fire-spouting Deva King, his voice like thunder.

"Your king has resisted the Han, and he has had his punishment from the Son of Heaven. Presently Wei-t'u-ch'i, who has long been a hostage in China, will arrive with troops and become your new king. Be careful that your irresponsible behavior does not mean the destruction of your country."

Before the assembly had recovered from the shock, Fu Chieh-tzu took out his sword and cut off the king's head.

⚜

2.

Wei-t'u-ch'i, who had been in Ch'ang-an, was informed by the Han court of his brother's death and ordered back to his native country.

It was some days, however, before he left Ch'ang-an.

"If I return to Lou-lan I will be killed by the Hsiung-nu and their friends. Fortunately there is a lake south of Lou-lan where the soil is rich. I request that Han soldiers be stationed there. With this show of strength, Lou-lan may be able to break free of the Hsiung-nu. Otherwise I have no confidence in my ability to govern the country."

Wei-t'u-ch'i submitted his petition and waited for an answer. At length the promise came from the emperor: a prefect and forty men would be stationed in the south.

Escorted from Ch'ang-an by Han soldiers, Wei-t'u-ch'i left the Jade Gate and crossed the dreaded White Dragon Dunes, where, it was said, there was no bird in the sky and no beast on the ground. When he saw from afar the forests that buried the shore of Lop Nor, two months had passed since the death of his brother.

A crowd gathered at the gate upon news of his arrival. They looked at their new king with cold eyes, however. As he passed through the gate, a boy not yet ten called out: "Do not betray the River Dragon."

The River Dragon was the god of the Lou-lan people.

When the new king had gone a little farther, an old woman shook her fist at him. "To leave Lou-lan is to die," she shouted.

The king did not understand the words of the boy and the old woman.

The royal mansion was guarded by Han soldiers. He was met by a number of princes and princesses whom he remembered, but their eyes too were cold.

Wei-t'u-ch'i had his first audience with the Han officer who had protected Lou-lan from civil war and the Hsiung-nu.

"Han soldiers will shortly be arriving at the lake to the south. We wish you to abandon this city as soon as possible and move the people of Lou-lan there."

This was indeed news. The king was stunned.

As long as it was by Lop Nor, Lou-lan would never be free from the depredations of the Hsiung-nu. To escape them and to submit to the Han, it must be moved farther south. Otherwise no number of Han troops could help. Such were the views of the Han rulers.

Wei-t'u-ch'i had asked for the stationing of Han troops, but it had not occurred to him that the whole country might be moved. Lop Nor was for Lou-lan a god, its ancestor, its life. The people of Lou-lan could not think of their country, of themselves, without Lop Nor, without the myriad branches of the Tarim that flowed into it, without the forests burying its shore, without the reeds and marshes bathed by the sun and rippled by the wind.

The first order of the new king was to summon every member of the royal family over ten and all the ministers and elders. He explained the grave circumstances facing Lou-lan. They had already heard from the Han officer. They had thought that Wei-t'u-ch'i was one of the conspirators, but his explanation was enough to correct the error and dispel their resentment.

The princes and ministers and elders had been arguing for days. No one was in favor of moving from Lop Nor, but the Han order could be called an ultimatum. Should they dismiss the order, knowing that to do so would mean the destruction of their country, or should they for the time being follow the wishes of the Han and occupy land farther south? These were the alternatives.

The final decision was to obey the Han, to leave Lou-lan behind, to build a new country in the south, to strengthen themselves under Han protection, and, when the opportunity came, to return to Lop Nor.

Every night for a month there were fires within the walls of Lou-lan, and ceremonies and banquets. People seemed to have forgotten sleep. Young and old walked the firelit streets of the city.

In the interval, the site for their new city was decided upon. It was in the wilderness to the south of a freshwater lake that was small out of all comparison with Lop Nor. As soon as the place had been selected, people (no one knew who had been first) began calling it Charkhlik, which meant "new water." They could not think of calling it Lou-lan. There was no Lou-lan away from Lop Nor, and there were no men of Lou-lan.

The twenty days between the decision and the actual move were busy ones for the people of Lou-lan. They did not think that they were leaving forever the land they had so labored to build. They could not have believed it if they had tried. As they had changed sides so many times before, they had an easy time changing again, from following the Hsiung-nu to living under the protection of the Han. Until the Han had completely driven the Hsiung-nu from the Western Marches, the men of Lou-lan would escape their attacks by moving south. They would hide behind the armies of the Han.

Eluding the eyes of the Chinese soldiers, the people of Lou-lan took their treasures and walked the shores of Lop Nor in search of places to hide them. Some ventured many *li* from the town. There was jade said to be found on moonlit nights in Khotan, there was rare and beautiful jade found in the dry bed of the Tarim River some *li* from the walls of Lou-lan. There were square wall hangings of cloth and there were cloth pouches. There were silk robes with a rich, soft sheen, and silk slippers. There were the horns of curious animals, and artifacts made from them. Shuddering at the cries of "the bull yak of the lake"—a bird with a strident cry like the braying of a donkey—some went deeper and deeper into the forest. Some climbed the great dead trees by the lake. These activities went on by day and by night.

When the people of Lou-lan had finished hiding their treasures, they formed bands to go from the town to Lop Nor, to the Tarim River, to its branches, to marshes thick with reeds, to dry channels white against the sky—in all these places they built altars and fires and prayed to their god, the River Dragon.

There were two incidents as the day approached for the people of Lou-lan to move some two hundred fifty *li* to the south, the day for them to abandon their town by Lop Nor, where their ancestors had lived for so long.

One was the death of an old princess. She was an unfortunate woman who had early lost her husband and whose son had been captured by the Hsiung-nu. She had long been bedridden, and on the morning set for the departure she died in a room of her mansion. Since she was a member of the royal family she must be buried with dignity. The departure of Lou-lan to begin its new history was thus postponed a day. The red-stringed cap which she always wore was placed on her head. She was dressed in a light robe, wrapped in a dark brown cloth, and laid in her coffin.

The funeral procession left the city. The coffin was carried to a hill about a half *li* away and lowered into a grave dug deep in the clay. When the grave had been filled, the attendants brought several large stones to mark it. The mourners lingered on, partly from sorrow for the old woman, partly because they would for a time be leaving Lop Nor, spread out now below them.

The other incident came that night, as if to overtake the first. It was the death of An-kuei's widow by her own hand, the death of the former queen.

It was suicide, of that there could be no doubt. Beautifully made up and dressed, she was found in bed by a maid. There was no sign of suffering on her face, but a leaf of poison was found in her mouth.

The most deeply grieved of all was the new king, Wei-t'u-ch'i. He had secretly hoped, if she was willing, to take his brother's beautiful young wife for his own queen. It had not been his hope alone. It had been the hope of the whole royal family, and of the whole Lou-lan nation. Wei-t'u-ch'i had of course said nothing. The young and inexperienced king had been immersed in the far more pressing problem of moving the city. He had meant to consult those about him once the move was made, and upon their consent to announce his betrothal.

But the widow of the former king had destroyed herself. The reason for her death was debated throughout Lou-lan. Some said that she had died from an excess of grief over the tragic death of the king, others that she had been sad at having to leave Lou-lan, where her husband was buried. Yet others said that she had sacrificed herself to this town, so soon to be abandoned. The truth was that no one knew. Her death was accepted calmly, however. No one thought it strange. What must happen had happened, and it only seemed strange that the obvious should have gone unnoticed. Now that she was dead, they knew that she could live nowhere except in Lou-lan—just as they could not think of the young queen away from Lop Nor.

The departure for Charkhlik, which had been postponed a day, now had to be postponed two days more. The queen's funeral was conducted with the greatest ceremony two days later. Her body was wrapped by maids in layer after layer of beautiful cloth, a turban was tied around her head, and she was laid in her coffin by Wei-t'u-ch'i himself. Upon the body he spread a beautifully figured cloth which he had brought back from Ch'ang-an.

They buried this coffin in the breast of a hill a short distance from the hill in which the old princess lay. The grave was a large one, and in it, packed in a number of boxes, were placed her treasures and the objects she used every day. A sheep was her one attendant. A sunset such as was to be seen only at Lou-lan, deep vermilion and purple and blue, spread behind the new grave.

A large tamarisk was brought from the shore of Lop Nor to mark the ground. Before it was placed a large stone basin for flowers. Wei-t'u-ch'i had no doubt that they would soon be coming back to pay their respects at the queen's grave.

At dawn the next day the people of Lou-lan gathered in the square before the gate, their goods loaded on thousands of horses and camels. As the sun from the far shore was beginning to turn Lop Nor rust red, they finished the last of their prayers to the River Dragon, and the head of the column moved off.

The long chain of men and horses and camels left the wall behind and turned north to skirt the marshes. Then, following a number of dry channels, it moved south. The end of the column was still at the town wall when the advance party had started into the desert.

A few minutes after the last of the column left the wall, three men turned back. One went through the gate and rode up to the house he was abandoning. He took from a shelf in the storeroom a work hatchet he had forgotten, and tied it at his waist. Then he remounted and rode off.

The second rode straight through the town to the gate on the opposite side, and on to the edge of the forest. He lifted the cover from the pit in which he had stored his treasures and put inside an heirloom, a small vase from the west. He replaced the lid, covered it with dirt, rolled a log over it, spread leaves, and otherwise made it quite impossible to detect the pit. Then he too remounted.

The last of the three who turned back had no particular aim. He rode down one deep alley and lane after another, went out through the same gate, and, after a last look back at the wall, turned his horse straight ahead and raced for the column again.

For two days Lou-lan was deserted. In those two days it

seemed to age by decades. This was partly because of the harsh winds, partly because the earthen walls had begun to break down. Ashen sand blew over the streets. The town seemed to fade; it took on the look of a ruin. On the evening of the third day there was at length a lull in the wind. Some hundreds of Han cavalrymen came in from the desert to occupy the town, and it was once more alive with the voices of men and the neighing of horses. On that day, Lop Nor was a muddy yellow, a turmoil of small waves.

3

During the eight decades between 77 B.C., when Lou-lan moved to Charkhlik, and A.D. 8, when Wang Mang deposed the last of the Former Han emperors, the Han had the better of the Hsiung-nu in the Western Marches. They appointed a warden of the Marches, stationed troops in key places, and were generally able to keep the city-states under control. There were great raids by the Hsiung-nu upon the Wu-sun and Turfan, but the Han were in the end able to expel the nomads from the Western Marches.

The people of Lou-lan broke new land by the shores of a fresh-water lake utterly different from Lop Nor, and built themselves a new city. They were not once attacked by the Hsiung-nu. For this reason, at least, the move to Charkhlik was a good one.

Some ten years after they had moved from Lou-lan, in 67 B.C., and in the reign of the Emperor Hsüan Ti, about a hundred men left Charkhlik for Lou-lan with about the same number of camels. They meant to bring back the treasures their people had buried there.

More than two-thirds of the hundred were in their twenties and above, men who had not once in those ten years forgotten the city of Lou-lan and the shores of Lop Nor. The others were too young to remember. Some of them had been born since the move to Charkhlik. Not a day had gone by but they had heard in prayers to the River Dragon the names Lou-lan and Lop Nor, but they had no concrete notion of those places. They could not imagine water in which there was salt and sand in which there was salt. They knew only that they must one day go back to live in that beautiful city. They believed it firmly, as if it were the fate that had been determined for their people by their god.

But the party met disaster. In the middle of the desert on the way to Lou-lan it was attacked by a band of Hsiung-nu, and half the camels and ten or more of the men were killed. The survivors did in the end make their way to Lou-lan, but they found their city a Han fortress. An endless procession was moving into the city by the lake and on to attack the Hsiung-nu, who were in possession of Turfan. The men of Lou-lan had no chance to dig up their treasures. They were not allowed inside the city, or even near it.

As they looked down from a sand hill upon the distant Lou-lan, the older men saw a different city from the one they had lived in. A howling wind seemed to crawl along the ground, and the sand rose in whirls and eddies. They did not think that they had seen such sand ten years before. The hills around the town, too, had changed shape, and seemed cold and distant. The water that had once been like crystal was muddy, the reeds had thinned, and even in sheltered coves the waves beat aimlessly at one another.

The River Dragon was angry, thought the men of Charkhlik who had once been the men of Lou-lan. They had to turn back, unable to dig up their treasures.

Some ten years later again, an old man of seventy who acted as supervisor of the water system set out on a camel for Lou-lan. He left alone and said nothing to anyone. There was a great stir when he disappeared.

On the tenth day, after a leisurely trip across the desert, he reached Lou-lan, which he had not forgotten even in his dreams. He dismounted and went through the gate. The city had fallen into disrepair, and there was not a person in sight.

Some fifty yards in from the east gate he came upon a fresh Chinese corpse. Fifty yards farther he came upon three Hsiung-nu lying face down, each with an arrow in his back. The old man walked on a few paces. He found another dead Chinese soldier. He stopped. He had heard the neighing of a horse, very near at hand.

He withdrew, remounted his camel, which he had left resting by the gate, and rode from the weird city. Swaying on the back of the camel, he rode for a whole day, and he dismounted when he knew that he was in the belt of marsh grasses near the southern extremity of the lake. He remembered that he had not accomplished any of his aims. He had brought back no treasures, he had not paid his respects at the ancestral graves, he had not gazed at the shores of Lop Nor. All this he had forgotten because of a few corpses in the city.

Having determined that the shore of Lop Nor could not be far away, he mounted his camel again. He came to a shore which seemed to be of Lop Nor. He dismounted, and what first came into his eyes as he looked out over the lake was a vermilion tower. There were several towers, but one was higher than the rest and the others raised their vermilion roofs about its skirts. The old man gazed on. He could not think that they were things of this world. He could only think that a colored picture had been spread there over the rippling waters of the lake.

He got on his camel and rode away, convinced that what he had seen in Lou-lan, and what he had seen upon the lake, were alike tricks. That he should be tricked twice in such quick succession—the River Dragon was angry.

He told no one in Charkhlik where he had been and what tricks he had had played on him. To pacify the River Dragon, the people of Charkhlik must return to their old home at Lou-lan as soon as they possibly could.

Although the scene which the old man came upon in Lou-lan was a most gruesome one, the reign of Hsüan Ti saw the greatest Han influence in the Western Marches. In 60 B.C. he made Chêng Chi warden of the Marches. After Chêng established his headquarters in Kucha, the small states generally accepted Han suzerainty. Commerce with China flourished, and almost every day caravans from the west passed to the north of Lou-lan.

The policies of Wang Mang, who in A.D. 8 usurped the throne, made light of the Western Marches. The Marches once more fell into confusion. The Hsiung-nu saw their opportunity and several of the city-states turned against the warden.

Charkhlik, however, remained solidly with the Chinese. The protection of the Han had made the people of Charkhlik forsake the land of their ancestors, and they could not bring themselves to change sides. If they were once more to fall under the Hsiung-nu, the move to Charkhlik would become meaningless. There were of course few who remembered Lou-lan, but everyone believed that giving up the old home had meant breaking forever with the Hsiung-nu. Whatever happened, Charkhlik must depend upon China, and its people must one day return to Lou-lan. The name Lou-lan had come to mean "City of the Return."

In China, the disturbances brought on by Wang Mang at length came to an end, and Kuang Wu Ti ascended the throne as the first of the Latter Han emperors. Han prestige was not what it had once been, however, and peace did not come easily to the Western Marches. The depredations of the Hsiung-nu only became more violent.

In A.D. 38 the third king of Charkhlik and the king of Yarkand, then becoming a dominant power in the Western Marches, sent a tributary mission to the Han. The ambassador took with him a petition that the Chinese be more aggressive in the Marches, and re-establish the wardenship, which had been discontinued because of the Chinese internal disturbances. The two countries, and their neighbors as well, were finding the levies of the Hsiung-nu cruel.

In A.D. 41 the king of Yarkand sent his own embassy to China, again asking that the wardenship be re-established. Unwilling to trouble himself with the Hsiung-nu, Kuang Wu Ti demurred and instead gave the warden's seal to the king of Yarkand. The Chinese bailiff of Tun-huang thereupon objected that the seal should not pass into the hands of a Tartar, and the emperor ordered the seal returned. The king of Yarkand was infuriated. He saw that the Han had no intention of managing the Western Marches, and he set out to forge a league with himself at its head.

Unable to submit in silence, the countries of the Western Marches banded together and reported these developments to the Han. The king of Charkhlik, along with the kings of seventeen other countries, sent a tributary mission to China. Each of the kings also sent a son to enter the Chinese service. The mission explained in great detail the condition of the Marches and asked once more that Kuang Wu Ti be more assertive. The eighteen emissaries described in turn how strongly they hoped to place themselves under the rule of the Chinese. The answer of Kuang Wu Ti, however, was equivocal. He rewarded the ambassadors, but did not accept the proffered services of the princes.

The men of Charkhlik fought back when the Yarkand invasion began. For the first time since the move from Lou-lan, they took arms to defend their city. They were defeated, however. They sent three embassies to explain the situation in the Marches. Kuang Wu Ti was indifferent. Charkhlik had therefore to consider other ways of saving itself. The king decided, along with the king of Turfan, to join the Hsiung-nu. Burning with resentment at the Chinese, the men of Charkhlik threw in their lot with the nomads. It was a hundred and twenty years since their ancestors had abandoned Lou-lan.

4

Kuang Wu Ti was succeeded by Ming Ti, who was too occupied with internal affairs to worry about foreign peoples. Like his predecessor, he closed the Jade Gate and the Yang Barrier, the doorways to the Western Marches. The Hsiung-nu ran unchallenged over the Marches. Charkhlik too had to bear the exactions of these overlords.

It was in the last years of Ming Ti's reign that the Han began once more to take an interest in the neglected Marches. The Northern Hsiung-nu were raiding the parts of China proper that lay west of the Yellow River. To defend their frontiers the Chinese had to establish themselves in the Marches. In A.D. 73 the Han court at length decided to strike out at the Hsiung-nu. Two generals, Pao Ku and Keng Ping, left the Chiu-ch'üan fortress, advanced far to the north across the desert, attacked the Hsiung-nu, and took Hami, their stronghold. When the military operation was over, Pao Ku sent Pan Ch'ao to establish communication with the countries of the Marches. Pan Ch'ao left the Jade Gate with thirty-six followers, and, after sixteen days in the desert, arrived at Charkhlik.

It was sixty odd years since the Wang Mang incident and the last Han embassy. It was the first time, moreover, that the people of Charkhlik had seen so many Chinese. The king entertained Pan Ch'ao warmly for some days, during which, however, a band of Hsiung-nu reached a point thirty *li* from the city. The king was forced to change his manner. From the change Pan Ch'ao guessed what had happened. Learning the Hsiung-nu position from the king of Charkhlik, he attacked and took the head of the leader.

Awed, the king swore his allegiance. Pan Ch'ao then made the rounds of the Marches, and commerce was opened for the first time in more than half a century. Charkhlik, Khotan, Bugur, Turfan, Urumchi, and the rest had all been victims of

Hsiung-nu violence. All were pleased to submit to the Han. The wardenship of the Western Marches was re-established, and the Han once more took active control of the region.

Only two years later, however, in A.D. 75, the Hsiung-nu with an army of twenty thousand men launched a campaign to take back the Marches. Thus began the war on which Pan Ch'ao staked his whole career. It was just before the great Hsiung-nu army headed south for a showdown with the Han that the king of Charkhlik led two thousand warriors to take Lou-lan, the old home of his people. Pan Ch'ao had set himself up in Bugur, which had a force of thirty thousand men, and made it his base for controlling the Western Marches. The hot-blooded king promptly decided to retake Lou-lan, so long a fortress of the Hsiung-nu. The people of Charkhlik were even more violent in their hatred of the Hsiung-nu than were the other peoples of the Marches. Several times every year the Hsiung-nu came down upon them. They locked their houses and hid under their floors, and turned the town over to Hsiung-nu savagery. They had to pay heavy tribute, and they had to submit to these ravages besides.

To the men of Charkhlik, Lou-lan no longer meant, as it had to their ancestors, "City of Return." It had become rather a place of revenge, where they must one day fall upon the Hsiung-nu and slaughter them. Two thousand Charkhlik warriors mounted their camels and horses and headed for the unknown land of their ancestral graves.

For the first three days they fought violent winds, but no one thought of turning back. At a point thirty *li* from Lou-lan they abandoned their camels and took to horses. That night they attacked Lou-lan. They had meant to scale the wall and strike at the Hsiung-nu encampments within, but the fighting began outside the city. Knowing that a night attack was probable, the Hsiung-nu waited for the Charkhlik force to approach and sent a shower of poisoned arrows from the walls. It was contest between bowmen on the walls and bowmen beneath. When a large number of Charkhlik warriors had fallen before the poisoned arrows, the Hsiung-nu attacked their flanks. The king was finally forced to order a retreat.

Under cover of darkness, the men of Charkhlik took to the desert and headed for home in disorganized bands. Some were struck down by the pursuing Hsiung-nu, others lost their way in the desert, and fewer than three hundred finally made their way back to Charkhlik. The king himself came crawling home, a mass of wounds, after everyone had given him up for lost.

Thus the assault on Lou-lan ended in disaster. It made the people of Charkhlik see, however, that they had no choice but to depend upon the Han. Ming Ti's control of the Western Marches was made difficult by the truculence of the Tartar peoples, who never seemed to know whether they were in a state of rebellion or a state of submission. Pan Ch'ao's life was spent in fighting, and through it all Charkhlik was the one state that remained firmly beside him. Indeed, it had no choice.

In 102 an aged Pan Ch'ao, who had spent half his life in the wars of the Western Marches, returned to Lo-yang, the Latter Han capital. The next warden was unsuccessful, and the countries of the Western Marches were once more cut off from Han China. The Hsiung-nu became more aggressive. In 107, during the reign of An Ti, the Marches were abandoned and the officers and soldiers of the wardenship withdrawn. There were three reasons: the way to the Marches was a long one, the Tartar peoples were unruly, and the cost of sending soldiers to the west was great. The Jade Gate and the Yang Barrier were once more closed. The Hsiung-nu emerged in control of the Western Marches. Lou-lan again became their fortress.

In 119, in the reign of An Ti, the Northern Hsiung-nu, in alliance with the countries of the Marches to the south of the T'ien-shan range, launched repeated attacks on the north-western provinces of China. Fearing an all-out attack, Ts'ao Tsung, the bailiff of Tun-huang, proposed that overtures be made to the countries of the Marches. More than a thousand soldiers under So Pan were sent to Hami. The first countries to recognize Han suzerainty were the countries that had suffered most under the Hsiung-nu, Turfan and Charkhlik.

The Hsiung-nu retaliated the next year, and, with the help of forces from Urumchi, destroyed Turfan and killed So Pan. The king of Charkhlik led a force to the assistance of the latter, but was defeated by the Hsiung-nu.

The king then asked help from Tun-huang, and the bailiff petitioned to have five thousand men sent against the Hsiung-nu. The Han court, however, failed to give its approval.

Later the court summoned Pan Yung, the son of that Pan Ch'ao who had been so successful in the Marches, and asked his views. He suggested the re-establishment of a force at Tun-huang and the despatching of five hundred men to Lou-lan under a deputy for the Western Marches. This plan aroused no more interest than the others.

In 124, upon order of An Ti, Pan Yung was at length despatched with five hundred men as deputy for the Western Marches. Charkhlik was the first state to join him.

Thus under Pan Yung the power of the Han once more reached into the Marches—only for a time, however. As Han enthusiasm for ruling the Marches began to wane, the Hsiung-nu came down again. Caught between the Han and the Hsiung-nu, and repeatedly the victim of the latter, Charkhlik was always prompt to join the Chinese when they came into the Marches. Always, however, the people of Charkhlik were betrayed. As they had been abandoned before, so they would be abandoned again.

※

In the days of Wu Ti, there had been some thirty small states on the fringes of the Tarim Basin. Caught between the Han and the Hsiung-nu, they followed now the one and now the other, in the meantime waging war among themselves. From about 280, when the period of the Three Kingdoms began, the number began to diminish and several strong successor nations emerged. Six of them came to hold territory out of all proportion to what they had held at the time of Wu Ti.

Large though they may have been, however, they were still vassals of larger foreign powers, among them the Hsien-pi who had supplanted the Hsiung-nu in the north; and they had to go on courting the Chinese authorities who were able to resist this new force.

In 324, in the reign of Ming Ti of the Eastern Chin, the Ch'ien Liang ruler who controlled the Tun-huang area sent a general across the Takla Makan to attack Kucha and Charkhlik. Both countries surrendered, and the king of Charkhlik sent tribute in the form of beautiful women.

In 382, during the reign of the Eastern Chin Emperor Hsiao Wu Ti, the king of Turfan and the king of Charkhlik visited the court of Fu Chien, a potentate in the northwest of China. The two kings from the Western Marches, wearing the court robes bestowed upon them by Fu Chien, were received in the Western Hall. Much impressed at the grandeur of the palace and the dignity of the ceremonies, they informed Fu Chien that they would like to appear annually with tribute. He declined the offer, saying that the road to the Western Marches was a long one. It was decided that tribute would be paid once every nine years. Soon afterwards the two countries were ordered by Fu Chien to act as guides for his viceroy, who was to lead seventy-five thousand men into the Marches. They were thus forced into conflict with their neighbors.

Presently Fu Chien was destroyed by the Eastern Chin. The upheaval brought confusion to the Western Marches.

A young Charkhlik general decided to attack Lou-lan, which had long been under the control of the Chinese. He would take advantage of the confusion to capture the city that had been the home of his distant ancestors, a city that by rights belonged to Charkhlik, and a city in which there would be troops of the ruined Fu Chien.

He started for Tun-huang with five hundred men. Along the way, he changed his course and headed toward Lou-lan. None of the five hundred knew what Lou-lan was to them.

They marched across the desert day and night, and on the last night, when they were but a half-day's march from the walls of Lou-lan, they were allowed to rest. As they started for Lou-lan the next morning, their young leader told them their mission. He also explained the deep meaning Lou-lan had for them. They had long respected his courage and his military prowess, and they did not consider going against his orders. They were stirred at the thought of taking back the home of their ancestors. Under such leadership they would surely accomplish the mission.

There had been a harsh wind from the time they set out, and it became even harsher as they approached their old city. At the command of their leader, the soldiers of Charkhlik pushed their way ahead, indeed were half-blown, mounts and all, through sand so thick that they could not see an inch before their faces. At length a great brown wall and a watchtower emerged from the sand.

The young officer took his place at the head of the band and himself cut down three guards at the gate. His men then closed ranks and marched inside. The fighting began immediately. They did not know the precise strength of the defending force, but it was considerably greater than they had expected. The attackers broke up into bands, which, however, were careful to maintain tight formations. No individual combat was allowed. The fighting spread to every house and every street and every tower and wall in the city.

Night came. To the fighters, it seemed to come with extraordinary swiftness. With night there was a lull in the wind. A third of the Charkhlik soldiers had fallen, but the defenders had lost several times that number.

There was a skirmish before dawn, and the fighting was over. The surviving defenders had apparently fled under cover of darkness. The Charkhlik soldiers walked a city littered with corpses. As invaders of Charkhlik were always doing, they went through every building in search of booty.

The young leader climbed to a watchtower with several of his men. The land which his ancestors had controlled six hundred years before was harsh and forbidding. It was surrounded by an ocean of sand, and the dunes were waves upon the ocean. The sand was a harsh white, like breaking waves.

The wind was blowing, though not as hard as the day before—blowing wisps of white into the air from the sides and caps of the sand waves. The wisps became a thin curtain of sand, moving from north to south.

How, he wondered, had his ancestors been able to live here, without river and without lake? Seeing a wooded belt far to the northeast, however, he thought it might perhaps contain a small lake.

Later he heard from a subordinate who had been disposing of corpses in the desert that there was a long knife-shaped lake in the forest. Perhaps, the man said, the narrow lake eventually joined a larger lake. The young leader gathered men to go to explore it. Knowing that no enemy reinforcements were likely to come, he was prepared to enjoy himself. The lake that drove like a blade through the forest was crystal clear and very shallow. It went on and on, and gradually widened. Occasionally there were flocks of birds.

Back in the city, the soldiers gathered around a wine cask they had found and began their victory banquet. Soon it was sunset, a richly colored sunset such as the men of Charkhlik had never seen before.

One soldier said that it was a bad omen. They should withdraw as soon as possible. The young leader could not deny that, to him also, it seemed ominous. They stayed another night nonetheless.

The next morning the soldiers of Charkhlik heard a strange howling. The wind had risen again, but it was not the wind they heard. It was a sound that came through the wind.

The young leader ordered a soldier to a tower. Just then the first arrow hit the side of a building and fell into the street. It was a long arrow, and after it a shower of arrows fell upon the stone paving. They came from a considerable distance, but it was not possible to determine the direction. Blown by the fierce wind, they struck the ground almost horizontally.

The soldier came down from the tower. The air was black with sand, and he had been able to see nothing. The leader himself went up the tower, but it was as the man had said.

The wind howled through a sky dark as night, and with it came that other sound—the angry howling of Lop Nor. The leader would probably have seen it the day before if he had gone a little farther.

He came down from the tower. The rain of arrows was heavier and the strange noise seemed nearer. He marched his men toward the gate, since they would be at a disadvantage fighting a large enemy within the walls. They were not quite fast enough, however. At the guardhouse they came upon a strangely clad troop making its way in. The soldiers of Charkhlik faced the enemy there inside the gate. Each with a long sword in hand, the men of the strangely clad troop feinted and lunged at them.

The soldiers of Charkhlik answered with their long spears. Sand began to descend on the battlefield like a waterfall. Both sides had to stop fighting. They could not keep their eyes open, and the sand penetrated the smallest holes in their armor.

The wind grew yet fiercer and the sand yet thicker. The sun was hidden, and the fighters could hardly make one another out.

The young leader had finally pushed his way through the gate with a number of followers. They could go no farther. The sandstorm was even worse than within the city. The soldiers of Charkhlik one by one joined their leader, and the band lay huddled against the wall. With them were a number of enemy soldiers who had been unable to go inside. The neighing of hundreds of ponies and the crying of camels came through the howling wind and waves.

The wind howled on for three days and three nights. Men and horses and camels were buried in the sand. The wall of the city was half buried.

The fighting had stopped as though it had never started. The soldiers of Charkhlik and the second invaders spent three days fighting sand instead.

When the wind died down on the fourth day, the young Charkhlik leader withdrew from the town, leaving scores of his followers buried in the sand. The other troop too left the little citadel in the desert, many of its number taken by the sand.

Having lost their horses, the soldiers of Charkhlik had to go back on foot. When they left Lou-lan the desert was still a chaos of sand eddies, but as evening drew on it fell quiet.

They were made sport of by the desert for some days more. They would hear the lively voices of their families nearby and what seemed to be the neighing of many horses. They would see before them groves in which there must be springs, but as they advanced the groves would disappear.

A month after his departure the young Charkhlik leader returned with a fifth of his men. They did not know who their strange adversaries at Lou-lan had been. Apparitions, perhaps—another prank of the desert? The young leader was never to know that he had met a patrol of the Jou-jan, a powerful tribe to the north.

Two years later he again visited Lou-lan at the head of troops. Lou-lan was buried in the desert, however. Only a watchtower here and there emerged from the sand. He went into the forest to look at the knife-shaped lake, but he found only a channel of white sand stretching through the forest like a sash. There was no water.

Lop Nor had disappeared, and Lou-lan was buried in sand. Some sixty years later Charkhlik went to war against Ta Wu Ti of the Wei, who ruled much of China. Defeated by soldiers sent from Liang-chou, Charkhlik became a Wei prefecture. Thus Lop Nor and Lou-lan and Charkhlik disappeared from history within a few years of one another.

5

In 399, during the reign of the Eastern Chin Emperor An Ti, the priest Fa-hsien with more than ten disciples set out from Ch'ang-an for India to learn Sanskrit and to study Sanskrit texts. His chronicle says of the Marches: "Beyond the Jade Gate is a desert belt, the home of malevolent spirits who stir up hot winds. No one has survived. There is no bird in the sky and no beast on the ground. There is nothing to close off the limitless prospect. He who seeks a landmark finds only the bleaching bones of men and animals to mark the way."

It is not clear whether Fa-hsien crossed the sands in which Lou-lan lay sleeping, or the land that had once been the shore of Lop Nor. It is not difficult to imagine, in any case, that he passed near Lou-lan.

In the T'ang Period, the priest Hsüan-tsang, who went to India under orders from the Emperor T'ai Tsung, brought the holy texts of Buddhism back to the T'ang capital after great hardships. He passed Lou-lan on his return.

In the *Great T'ang Chronicle of the Western Marches* there is this brief entry: "More than four hundred *li* farther is the ancient country of Tu-lo. It has long been abandoned and the citadel is in ruins. More than six hundred *li* to the east is the ancient country of Charchan. The walls are firm, but there is no sign of man or fire. More than a thousand *li* to the north and east is the ancient land of Lou-lan."

Hsüan-tsang saw two uninhabited cities in the desert, but of Lou-lan he had nothing to say. The city was no doubt buried deep in the sand. This was more than a thousand years ago, in the year 645.

✤

In the twentieth century Lou-lan awoke from its long sleep and once more appeared on the pages of history.

The colors on the map had changed many times. No one, however, had paid much attention to Central Asia, where Lou-lan slept. Few had ventured into that lifeless desert belt.

In 1900 the buried city of Lou-lan was uncovered after more than a thousand years, by the Swedish explorer Sven Hedin. It took a great deal of argument to determine that the site was in fact that of Lou-lan. And to determine the position of Lou-lan the mystery had to be solved of Lop Nor, which had once washed near Lou-lan but which had since disappeared.

As its inhabitants had been unable to think of Lou-lan away from Lop Nor, so modern scholars were unable to think of the two apart. If the ruins found by Hedin were those of Lou-lan, Lop Nor should be near them, now as then. What had happened? Lop Nor must be chosen from among the lakes of the desert, even if it be but a sad vestige of old Lop Nor. The secret must be unraveled of how it had moved.

As it became clear that the site was indeed Lou-lan, a new theory came to be accepted: Lop Nor moved south and north in cycles of fifteen hundred years. Because sedimentation and the workings of the wind brought changes in the course of the Tarim River, Lop Nor moved from south to north and from north to south every fifteen hundred years.

In 1927 Hedin, then sixty-two, gathered a large number of experts for his fourth journey into the Western Marches. Known officially as the Scientific Expedition to the Northwestern Provinces of China, the company was composed of eighteen German and Swedish scholars, ten Chinese, and native porters and cooks.

On this fourth journey Hedin again visited Lou-lan. One day he was following a channel that had been dry since about the fourth century. There, where water had flowed in the days of Lou-lan and where for so many centuries there had been none, water was again beginning to flow. Because Lop Nor had shifted, Lou-lan had been left to the sand. Water was coming to a few of the dry stream beds, and with it plant and animal life. Water would come in time to the scores of channels that were still dry, and the myriad forms of life would come with it.

That day Hedin found two coffins in the desert. One was on top of a hill, the other was at the foot of a hill some distance away. He has described the second discovery in considerable detail.

❦

"Two of our hawk-eyed boatmen discovered another grave from the top of the *mesa*. This one was on the eastern side of the *mesa*, on the top of a quite small *mesa* at the foot of the big one.

"Leaving the mass grave to the peace we had so heartlessly and violently disturbed, we went down to the solitary resting-place, and as I saw that there would be no more paddling that day, I ordered camp to be pitched just to the south-west of grave no. 2. But all the men begged to be allowed to stay with us till the investigation was over, and I could not refuse them that ghoulish pleasure.

"The small *mesa* with the single grave ran from north-east to south-west. It was only 41 feet long by 12 feet wide. Its summit was 29 feet above the surface of the water and 24 feet above the surrounding earth. From the top of the big *mesa* one could see that the hillock contained a grave, for a post of tamarisk wood stood on it, which could not be natural, as the tops of *mesas* are always bare and sterile.

"The isolated post invited digging, and the men got to work. But the clay of this *mesa* was almost as hard as brick, and in the process of transformation into clay-slate. So an axe was fetched up from the landing place and the men cut their way through the hard material. The grave was rectangular. It was quite close to the north-western flank of the *mesa*, and the clay wall was only a foot thick on the top, lower down 2 feet. At a depth of 2 feet 3 inches the diggers struck a wooden lid, which was exposed first with the axe, and then with the spade. It consisted of two very well-preserved boards 5 feet 11 inches long. The breadth of the lid was 1 foot 8 inches at the head and 1 foot 5½ inches at the foot, and the thickness of the boards was 1½ inches. The head lay towards the north-east.

"As soon as the lid had been cleaned, and we had found that the coffin exactly fitted its clay case and that it was impossible to lift it out without enlarging the hole that had been dug, we decided to clear away the clay wall on the north-western side, which cost us both time and labour. But at length the last obstacle was removed, and the coffin could be carefully coaxed out and lifted up on to the top of the *mesa*.

"The shape of the coffin was characteristic of that watery region. It was just like an ordinary canoe, with the bow and stern sawn off and replaced by vertical cross-boards.

"The two boards which formed the lid had been lifted even before the outer wall of the *mesa* was broken through. We eagerly awaited the sight of the unknown dead who had slept so long undisturbed. But instead we found only a blanket in which the corpse had been shrouded and which hid it completely from head to foot. The shroud was so brittle that it broke up into dust at the touch. We removed the part which concealed the head—and we saw her in all her beauty, mistress of the desert, queen of Lou-lan and Lop Nor.

"Death had surprised her young, and loving hands had enshrouded her and borne her to the peaceful mound within which she was to rest for nearly 2,000 years till the children of an age then far distant should wake her from her long sleep.

"The skin of her face was like hard parchment, but its shape and features were not changed by time. She lay with eyelids closed over eyeballs that had fallen in hardly at all. About her lips a smile still played that the centuries had not extinguished, and which rendered the mysterious being still more appealing and attractive. But she did not betray the secrets of her past, and her memories of the variegated life of Lou-lan, the spring green about the lakes, river-trips by boat and canoe, she had taken with her to the grave.

"She had seen the garrison of Lou-lan march out to battle against the Huns and other barbarians; the war chariots with their archers and spearmen; the great trade caravans which had passed through Lou-lan and rested in its inns, and innumerable camels carrying bales of China's precious silk westward along the Silk Road. And surely she had loved too, and had been loved. Perhaps she had died of grief. But of all this we could know nothing.

"The length of the coffin inside was 5 feet 7 inches, and the unknown princess had been a little woman, about 5 feet 2 inches.

"In the afternoon sunshine, Chen and I began a fairly minute examination of the clothing in which she had been committed to earth. She wore on her head a turban-like cap, and round it a single band. Her body was covered with a linen cloth (possibly of hemp), and under this there were two similar coverings of yellow silk. The breast was covered by a square red piece of embroidered silk, with, under it, yet another short linen garment. Under this again she wore a thin skirt, drawers and woven silk slippers. Her waist was encircled nearest the body by a kind of girdle.

"We took away samples of all these garments, some—the headdress and slippers, for example—entire, and a purse of beautifully patterned silk in many colours. Outside the coffin, at its head, we found a rectangular four-legged food table with a low rim; a red-painted wooden bowl and the skeleton of a whole sheep—provisions for the traveller on her journey to another world."

⚘

We need not inquire whether the coffin Hedin found was that of the young queen who killed herself on the eve of the departure from Lou-lan. Her death was a mystery, and why should we want to know more? It is enough that for fifteen centuries Lou-lan lay buried under the sand, that its site and the position of Lop Nor were forgotten, and that both were presently brought to light again.

Lop Nor is returning to the site of Lou-lan. A half century has gone by since Hedin discovered Lou-lan, and in that time the waters of Lop Nor have continued to advance. Even now they are advancing. It will be some decades yet before they reach Lou-lan. But Lop Nor is returning, and with it the River Dragon who was the god of Lou-lan. Perhaps, indeed, he has already returned.

The Sage

Translated by
James T. Araki

Many nomadic peoples once lived in Central Asia. Some were independent while others joined in leagues to consolidate their strength. They lived in tents, and their many villages were scattered across the broad grasslands, the secluded valleys and slopes of closely layered mountain ranges. The nomads whom the Persians knew as the Saka and the Greeks as the Scythai have been best covered in the histories. The Saka were active between the seventh and first centuries before Christ. In the third century their land was invaded by the armies of Alexander the Great, but the mighty Alexander could not humble this nomadic race, whose people were skilled at archery and cavalry warfare. The league of Saka tribes soon began to fall apart, and they gave up their dominant position to those newcomers, the Hsiung-nu or Huns.

This story begins in the mid-sixth century B.C., when the Saka had not yet come together as a people but were divided into many tribes, constantly at war with one another.

⚑

North of the T'ien-shan Mountains and between the Kungey Alatau and Terskey Alatau ranges was a broad valley inhabited by a tribe of some three thousand Saka. They lived in tents or nondescript earthen houses that showed something of their nomadic past. Their ancestors had wandered the vast areas north of the T'ien-shan as far as the upper reaches of the Ob' and Yenisey rivers in constant search for pastures. They had settled in this valley several generations before and there they hunted, farmed and herded.

The valley was a grass-grown expanse bounded on the south by the Terskey Alatau Range, a virtual wall of towering peaks, their summits always snow-covered, as far away as the eye could see. The Kungey Alatau Range along the northern fringe was a similar stretch of peaks whose slopes, however, inclined gently toward the valley; the far-reaching skirts, brown and barren, evoked a sterile bleakness, though at sundown an eerie beauty would overspread them.

The village was on a rise, a cluster of low hills in the center of the valley. Some houses stood on the crests, others in the folds of the hills. The village roads twisted along the undulating terrain. Luxuriant trees stood alongside the roads and everywhere about the dwellings, and from afar appeared to coalesce into a dense, dark forest. There would be snow for about a month; but the climate was otherwise mild, and there was ample rain. In May, the melting snow would rush down the mountainsides until the two rivers that flowed along the foothills of the two ranges brimmed over. The valley would be inundated, but the water never rose as high as the village.

There were many other secluded valleys in the vast area between the T'ien-shan and Altay mountains; there the many Saka tribes had their villages and grazed their herds. This Saka tribe could not have found a better place in which to settle. In their valley the climate was mild, and the soil fertile, and there were rich pastures. It could easily be defended against invaders.

The only disadvantage was the limited supply of water—only one spring, at the foot of a knoll that marked the southwest corner of the settlement. The spring, which never stopped flowing, was enclosed in a huge dome built of stone and earth. The Sage held the key to the gates, which would be closed shortly after sunset and reopened at the first light of dawn. The villagers could draw water whenever the gates were open. But everyone, from the chief on down to the lowly herder, was allowed to fill only one jar. That was the daily amount apportioned to each member of the tribe. Everyone was treated equally.

Men and women carrying their jars stooped low to pass through the narrow entrance. They would humble themselves, their heads touching the ground, before the altar of their god, bow to the Sage, who sat in the small grotto beside the altar, and then descend the spiraling stone steps. The stairway was dark, and the dozen or so steps had to be negotiated carefully. The darkness about the pool was equally profound. Their jars filled, they would take the stone pathway along the edge to the opposite side of the pool and leave by an exit at the head of another stairway.

Although the villagers entered the dome daily, they had no distinct impression of its interior; they were aware only of a cold stone cavern with an abundant spring. The cavern was a place of mystical darkness, and the air within was always chilly.

The spring was sacred. Its water nourished the body as well as the spirit. The spring was their god, and the Saka of this village were content with their daily jar of water and never wished for more. Had anyone been tempted to draw more, he could easily have done so, for the Sage, who guarded the spring, was blind. But this had never happened. The villagers at once venerated and dreaded the spring and its aged guardian.

Naturally a jar of water was not enough for an adult's daily needs. Yet because everyone from infants to the aged was entitled to the same amount, a family would have enough water to drink and a surplus for raising vegetables and other uses, though not enough to water animals. Their horses and sheep were set to grazing along the bank of the great river at the foot of the Terskey Alatau Range, more than ten *li* away. There they were tended by the younger tribesmen, who took turns living with them.

Insufficiency of water caused hardship, and yet it was a blessing. There had been no discord for several decades, whereas other tribes were frequently beset by disputes over tribal leadership. Here no one had reason to envy or resent others. Everyone was satisfied with a small allotment of water from the sacred spring. Because there was little water, there were no aggressors. Although the many Saka tribes would join together in a league when they were threatened by other nomadic races, they were otherwise at war with one another. Having only one spring, this tribe was never drawn into conflicts. In the eyes of other tribes their elysian valley was quite uninviting.

It was the end of June of a year long forgotten. The house of the chieftain was astir as the villagers prepared to welcome the chieftain's younger brother, who would be returning from a Saka tribe in the upper reaches of the Yenisey. The youth, still an infant, had been sent as a hostage twenty-seven years before. He had grown up in the faraway village. News of his return came some days before.

From morning the men of the tribe were busy preparing a banquet in front of the chieftain's house; they carpeted the ground with sheepskin, set up many candles, and assembled an assortment of musical instruments. The women readied vats of wine, cooked the food, and decorated the site with flowers. All day there was the tantalizing odor of mutton.

At dusk the youth came riding alone into the village. His people were surprised, for they had thought he would be guarded closely by escorts. With a sword at his side and a bow and a quiver of arrows slung over his back, he seemed proud but somehow strange to a people who had not borne arms for many generations. He was surrounded by the village elders, eager to study a man who had been a mere infant when they delivered him to that village in the upper Yenisey. There was not one among them who did not exclaim in admiration at his piercing eyes and shoulders broader and more powerful than any of which their own young men could boast.

The youth walked up to his brother and greeted him in the way customary among his adoptive people. His movements were brisk, and there was dignity in his carriage.

Then he searched for his parents. When he learned they had both died ten years before he again followed the custom of his adoptive people, kneeling and lifting his gaze to the sky. His face registered grief, but fleetingly. He stood and took the seat designated for him. Only moments later, however, he was obliged to stand up once more, for the venerable Sage, keeper of the spring, was being led up the path toward them.

The Sage was feeble and had to be helped. The air had become charged the moment he was sighted at the bottom of the rise. Everyone stood in awe of him. He seldom left his hut near the spring, but on this night he had come to bless the youth, who shared the blood of their chieftain.

The youth faced the Sage and repeated the words uttered by one of the elders: as a member of this tribe he would honor the god of the spring and abide by his will; like the others, he would beg to be given his daily jar of water; he vowed never to be wanton in the use of water, for every drop was blessed. Thus in the presence of the Sage he took the oath that was required of every member of the tribe.

When the youth stood, so did the Sage. Again attended by several escorts, the Sage left by the same sloping path. Everyone had been awed by the encounter with holiness. Everyone stood hushed, transfixed, until the Sage had disappeared.

But the youth told himself that the old man who held absolute control over the water was a stupid, lifeless cripple. His face with its sunken eyes was ugly. He had not said a word and this reluctance to speak was puzzling. Could the old man have heard the oath he had been compelled to utter? Was he not only blind but deaf as well? It was odd in the first place that a spring should be worshiped as a god. He had grown up where water was always plentiful, where a tributary of the Yenisey cradled the village in a curve of its flow. The many springs in the village were used mainly for watering the animals. There were wells. If more water was needed, more wells were dug.

The youth was accustomed to the worship of fire. He had never known a people who worshiped a spring. He had been told that the people of his own tribe had unusual customs. He became aware of the annoyance he must endure.

The banquet was dreary, he thought. The wine was served in such scanty portions that no one could get drunk. The village girls danced, but they cast no sinuous, erotic shadows. The youth missed the altar of fire and sensuous tongue-like flames which he had learned to associate with festivity. The banquet was meant to gladden him, to make him forget the grim years he had spent in captivity. Yet he thought it dull, and it ended early.

On the following day, the village elders gathered in council to determine the authority to be vested in the youth, now a member of the chieftain's household, and the role he would play in tribal affairs. The youth was present, and he told the council what had crossed his mind the night before.

"Can we not have another spring?" he asked. "Wherever there is one spring there are bound to be others. I know this from experience. We can easily find out by digging in the vicinity of the spring."

Never before had the elders heard such profanation. One of them said he regretted having lived so long, that he must endure such blasphemy. A spring in addition to that in which their god dwelt! Surely, another added, their god of the spring was angered that they had brought such a man into their midst. With that the meeting ended.

The council convened again three days later. The youth came forth with a new suggestion: would they consider a ration of two jars of water daily? "I've noticed how the spring is always brimming when the gates are opened in the morning even though it drops somewhat at night. It might not be inexhaustible, I suppose. But I doubt if it would run dry simply because we drew twice what we're drawing now."

Here again, the youth's proposal had the effect of causing the elders to call an end to the meeting. The wretch was dissatisfied with the god's gift of water and was asking for more! A jar of water was the amount determined by their god; and gods had their reasons. The thought of questioning was itself frightening. The tribe lived in tranquillity because it obeyed the god's commandment. The chieftain trembled with rage, and the elders agreed that they must not meet again until the youth was freed from the demon that had possessed him.

Ten days passed, and the council met for a third time. The youth meanwhile had decided to present the council with new knowledge about the spring: the Sage, who was entrusted with the key to the spring, was in truth an aged cripple of no account. He was blind and, as the youth had noticed on their first meeting, he was also deaf, and he uttered nothing that resembled words. Although he mumbled something over and over all day long, no one knew what it meant. The Sage was not only blind, he might well be a deaf-mute. A virtual cripple, he could not himself open and close the gates to the spring. That task was performed by a seventeen-year-old girl, an orphan who had been placed in the service of the Sage some years before and had been living with him since. The only advantage the Sage could claim over the others was age. No one knew how old he was; even in the earliest childhood recollections of the village elders, he was the Sage who kept the key to the spring.

At this third meeting of the council, the youth spoke again.

"The Sage who keeps the key to the spring cannot see, and he cannot hear, and he cannot talk. Of what use is he? He should open and close the gates at dawn and nightfall, but he no longer does that himself. He merely sits in the grotto beside the entrance. It is the only work he does—if indeed we can call that work. Because he performs this curious job the villagers revere him and feed him. He should be pitied, not revered. He retains his job only because of his incapacity."

The youth was cut off by a chorus of angry shouts. Sensing peril, he sprang to his feet, but in an instant was flung to the ground. A host of men pummeled and whipped him until he no longer stirred.

He regained consciousness in a grass-covered field far from the village. Though he had not been expected to survive, his vigor had raised him from the abyss of death.

It was dark night. He felt someone applying a medicinal herb to his inert body, moving from one lesion to another. Pain stabbed a line of agony over his body. He lapsed into unconsciousness.

When again he revived, he found himself lying in a herder's hut. A girl brought him food. Several days went by before he recognized the girl who had saved him; it was she who lived with the Sage. Whenever there was a death in the village, she went out to the field where the body lay and conducted rites on behalf of the Sage. The youth had had the good fortune to be found while he still lived.

His wounds healed, he departed for the village far to the north where he had grown up in captivity. The girl bade him farewell. When he thanked her, she replied that she was dedicated to serving their god and had merely carried out his wish. She seemed stern and impassive—typical of religious zealots, he thought—but he sensed a tenderness that had compelled her to restore him to life rather than abandon him.

The villagers talked often about the heretic youth. None of them knew that he had survived and returned to the faraway tribe. The Saka customarily abandoned their dead in the fields to be preyed upon by beasts and birds, and they had thus disposed of the youth. They did not believe that he was truly a member of the chieftain's family. They were convinced that the tribe in the upper Yenisey basin had sent them a heinous substitute.

⚘

Just a year later, calamity befell the village. It was assailed by some three hundred mounted invaders. They galloped up and down the roads of the village, trampling all that lay in their path. Then they regrouped before the chieftain's house.

The village elders had been ordered to gather there. They were astounded when they saw the leader of the mounted invaders; it was the youth they thought they had pummeled to death a year earlier.

The council was forced to accept every demand set forth by the youth. He proclaimed himself chieftain in place of his elder brother, and the council acknowledged him as their leader.

The youth reduced his brother, who had shown him no pity, to a lowly herdsman, and he meted out similar fates to those elders who had willed his death. He appointed new village leaders. They were all young men.

That night a blazing altar was set up before the house of the new chieftain. The soldiers had appropriated wine from the villagers and now abandoned themselves to carousal. The flame, blazing deep into the night, was the focus of crazed jubilation. The villagers had never known such uproarious revelry. None could sleep that night.

The village underwent bewildering changes. The new council approved resolutions which before would have been considered outrageous.

The daily quota for water was increased to two jars, with the promise that it might eventually be increased to three, perhaps four, so long as the spring remained unaffected. On the day the new policy was proclaimed, no villager exercised his right to draw water. Only soldiers from the other tribe, now stationed in the village, were seen at the spring, drawing water freely.

The altar was torn down, and the Sage was forbidden access to the spring. The villagers had seen the girl lead him daily to his place at the entrance; and now he would no longer be guardian of the spring.

The youth thought he should make an example of the Sage and so hasten conversion of the villagers to a way of life in which water would be plentiful. For his crime of having deceived the villagers, that useless wretch, blind and deaf and dumb, deserved to be made a beggar, to wander the streets begging food. Despite his intentions the youth did nothing, for it would have been unkind to the girl who lived with the Sage. Though he forbade him the spring, he let him remain in his hut. He wished, however, to separate the girl from the Sage and bring her to his own tent. The girl refused.

"The Sage has his god-given task," she said, "and I must perform it for him."

"And what is that?"

"The gates to the spring must be locked at night and opened at dawn."

The youth thereupon decided to relieve the Sage of his only remaining task. He issued a decree that the gates to the spring should always be open. But wolves began prowling about the village at night. In one attack, several persons were killed. The villagers, reluctant as they were even to draw their full ration of water, did not dare approach the spring in the deep of night. The victims were all soldiers from the other tribe.

The young chieftain, unafraid, went out late in the night to inspect the spring. In the company of several archers, he scaled the dome and peered into an aperture through which moonlight beamed, casting a pale light on the poolside. There he saw wolves, some curled up on the ground, a few standing with their heads raised proudly, and several pacing about restlessly.

He must have the gates closed at nightfall lest the spring become a haunt of wolves. The decree was withdrawn, and the Sage was again made the keeper of the gates. The young chieftain found himself unable to keep his thoughts from the girl who had saved his life.

Almost half a year went by before most villagers, no longer fearing the wrath of their god, were bold enough to draw two jars of water daily. Once they saw that there would be no divine punishment, they went to the spring regularly. Throughout the day there was a constant stream of men and women bearing jars. Yet not everyone adapted to the new way. There were still a few, mostly elderly, who took only one jar of water. They were the ones who always brought food to the door of the Sage's hut before going on to the spring. Once inside the dome, they would touch their heads to the ground as if the altar were still there, and offer prayers of thanks before descending the stairs which led to the spring, the dwelling place of their god.

In time the village changed. The streets took on life as more and more men and women went outdoors to pass the time of day. There was laughter, singing, and shouting.

The youth made the rounds of the village daily. In the beginning he would meet with reproachful glances, never with suggestions of fondness. In half a year, however, there was a remarkable change. The youth was greeted warmly wherever he went.

The men and women of the village worked with far greater diligence than before, and they were sprightly. Young people formed groups of their own and gathered nightly at one house or another. The air would be filled with song and music. There was feasting and drinking. Wine was now unrestricted and it was the fare at all gatherings.

Work hard during the day and devote the evening to pleasure, the drudgery of work forgotten: this was the ideal the young chieftain had sought to instill in the tribe, and he had done it in a matter of six months. In less than a year he could despatch the soldiers homeward. He no longer needed them.

Not long after, caravans began coming, and life in the village became still brighter, even festive. Caravans from distant tribes had passed the village by because they could not get water; now they came regularly from unknown parts. The villagers set up a bazaar, where they exchanged their pelts and carved objects for rare merchandise.

The allotment of water had been doubled, and this simple act had led to the remarkable change. Now there was wealth and there was gaiety. In the course of that year there were other unprecedented happenings: two cases of adultery, seven of theft, and thirteen of assault. As the young chieftain investigated he became aware of subtler transgressions. A few villagers, all young, were drawing three or four jars of water daily from the spring. Some of them made a trade of drawing as much water as possible to peddle among the alien merchants and their own tribespeople as well. Most discommoding to the chieftain as he sought to adjudicate this matter was the prevalent use of notes that were negotiable for water. A palm-sized piece of parchment was the equivalent of a jar of water, and some had accumulated dozens, even hundreds of them. Doubtless there had been days when a villager had not needed a second jar of water. Being entitled to two, perhaps he regarded the undrawn second jar as a redeemable loss, and devised the currency that was now in wide use. In terms of water there were now the rich and the poor. The extremely poor had already forfeited their right to draw water from the spring for as long as six months.

The youth decided to return the Sage to his station beside the entrance. Blind or not, a guardian would be better than no guardian at all. But the Sage was no longer effective. His presence meant nothing to the youths of the village. Neither spring nor Sage retained anything of the former power to inspire dread and obedience.

In the next six months, there were more than a dozen instances of adultery, and there were two killings. An accurate count could not be kept of such lesser crimes as theft and assault, so commonplace had they become. What disturbed the young chieftain most, however, was the wantonness that now pervaded the village. Young men and women gathered nightly to dance, and every dance, every song, was lascivious. A few among the elderly condemned what seemed to them a deplorable trend. The others could not be censorious, for they, too, had misbehaved.

🙢

The youth had been chieftain almost two years when two incidents brought the tribe into conflict with a neighboring tribe. A youth from the village had robbed and killed a merchant from the other tribe; and the wife of one of the villagers had run off with a young man from the other tribe. Such affairs would have been unthinkable in the past.

The differences could not be resolved peacefully. The villagers agreed to an indemnity for the death of the merchant but they insisted that the adultress be returned to them. The other tribe refused.

For the first time the young men of the village left the valley to ride into battle; a few days later only a tenth of them came straggling back. This outcome should not have been surprising, for the men had been given little training as soldiers. The battle lost, the tribe ceded a large fertile area along the northern foothills to the victors.

The young chieftain could not accept this humiliation. He had sought help from the tribe in the upper Yenisey basin in order to become tribal chief. He went to them again.

He ordered every able-bodied male in the village to take up arms and he merged them with the great army that came to his assistance. He rode into battle at the head of the army.

The war raged for more than a month, and victory followed victory. The young chieftain, an exceptional commander, was given credit for every victory.

Having negotiated the enemy's surrender, the young chieftain returned at the head of a victorious band. There were only women to greet them. They frantically sought out their husbands and sons, for more than half the men of the village had been killed. Cries of joy mingled with mournful wailing.

The chieftain immediately announced that the entire village would be turned over to a great victory celebration. He could not have had his victory without the help of the mighty army of the other tribe, which would soon be coming into the village. He must express his gratitude. Though the tribe had lost many men, elation over victory was everywhere. The villagers began drinking even before sundown and were soon raising senseless shouts and shrieks. Not only its people but the village itself seemed drunk. A messenger rode up and informed the villagers that the great army would likely arrive late in the night.

Although the youth was in high spirits he was badly wounded. He wanted to be nursed by the girl who lived with the Sage. He called her to his tent. The girl came and applied a medicinal herb to his wounds, as she had done before. The youth felt an almost mystic tenderness in the movements of her hands. Such tenderness must be an expression of love, he thought.

Passion had been restrained by gratitude, but now it flowed uncontrollably. Whatever might come, he would keep her in his tent. Sensing his determination, she said to him: "I am entrusted with a very special task. The Sage has made me the gatekeeper to the spring where our god resides. Let me show you the key."

She took out from the bosom of her dress an arrow-shaped object. The sensuous curve of her breast was disturbing.

How different she was! She maintained her belief in the god of the spring. And she believed that keeping that key was her god-given mission. Twice she had healed his wounds with such tenderness as could only signify love. Yet she took no notice at all of his desire.

"This is a very special night for me," he said. "It is the night of my triumphal return from war. You must stay with me just this one night."

The girl looked up. An unusual determination made her strangely alluring. Her reply was firm.

"I must refuse even at the cost of my life. Our god commands that the gates be locked, and the Sage obeys. But the Sage is infirm. I keep the key because I perform the task for him. Surely you remember how our god showed his wrath when the gates were kept open. The village was attacked by wolves. The god allows no one to draw water at night. I must not stay, for the troops expected tonight will ride straight to the spring. I must lock the gates."

The youth was not listening. He took her to his bed by force.

❧

"You would not want to leave me now," he said afterwards.

"It is true." The girl's eyes were filled with tears. "I have been telling myself I must escape, but I cannot."

She looked at the key, on a small table.

"I know I must take the key and leave. I have told myself this. But I cannot interrupt such bliss! Death would be the easier."

Soon night came, with its veils of darkness. The village was alive with shouting and drumbeats. But time passed quietly within the tent. The girl was brought to her senses by a neighing of countless horses. She recoiled from the chieftain's arms, took the key, and ran from the tent. It was long past the hour to lock the gates.

The girl ran as fast as she could, over the winding and twisting road through the village. She looked like an apparition. It seemed as if her soul had left her body and taken flight.

When she came within sight of the spring she cried out in despair. The dome was ringed by hundreds of horses.

The girl tried to block the narrow entrance, but was shoved aside by soldiers making their way to the spring. She knew that there was no point in closing the gates now, and for a time ran aimlessly about. Then she scaled the dome and peered through the aperture at the top. The spring was quite unlike the one she was accustomed to. As on the night when the young chieftain discovered the pack of wolves, moonlight streamed through the aperture to cast a pale light over the spring. She could not believe her eyes. The pool had been drained, and a huge boulder at the bottom lay exposed. Several soldiers had leaped onto the boulder and were lading what little water remained. The boulder appeared to be blue—due perhaps to the effect of moonlight, she thought. That was not so. The stone pathway along the pool's edge, now suddenly risen far above the water, was not the same color. Only the flat-surfaced boulder in the center of the pool was blue, a blue that was supremely clear and brilliant as if blended with moonlight.

The girl saw the huge boulder sway gently, and the soldiers standing on it spread out their arms to balance themselves. But the next instant the boulder had tilted and the soldiers had vanished, and water was gushing into the pool, swirling about the blue boulder. Filling swiftly, the water in moments engulfed the boulder, and rose to the level of the rocky ledge, and then beyond. The cries of the men clustered about the stairway became hollow, muted. As the girl slid down the dome, she felt a great swaying. With unbelievable swiftness the gushing water had filled the dome.

The girl ran. She would have gone to the hut which she shared with the Sage, but there was no time. She knew that she must flee to high ground. As she ran she heard the roar of raging water.

The horses were beginning to move, neighing, a rampaging herd. The girl turned abruptly toward her hut. If she could get the key into the Sage's hand, she thought, the spring might somehow be brought under control. But she was forced to turn back by several swift flows that were forming into rivers. The moon took on a strange reddish cast. The piercing cries of all the living creatures in the valley filled the air above.

Five months later, the valley between the two Alatau ranges was filled to brimming by water that issued from the spring. The village was submerged, its people too. They had fled to higher ground as the low-lying areas were inundated. Eventually they could flee no more and perished. It was only two and a half years after the youth had become the tribal leader.

As the valley brimmed with water, a large peak on its southwest shore disintegrated, half of it sliding away in an instant. This left a breach through which water drained out of the valley, leaving the water level constant.

A few survived the cataclysm. When it was all over, three men and two women were seen on the shore of the new lake. The Sage was one of them. We cannot account for his survival, but he did indeed survive. He continued to mumble the same meaningless sounds. The other survivors, all from distant tribes, thought the ordeal must have driven him mad. One of them, a middle-aged woman, however, listened closely. She understood what he was saying: "Do not touch the blue rock, the blue rock of the god." From years before, scores of years before, that is what the Sage had been saying, quite as if he had committed only those words to memory. The woman was from a small tribe in the Altay region; doubtless the old Sage spoke the language of her tribe.

※

The lake whose origin we have described is the Issyk-kul' in the Kirghiz Socialist Republic. Approximately the size of Lake Biwa, it is secluded amidst the T'ien-shan Mountains. The outlet mentioned in our story is the Chu River, which has carved out the Chu Gorge and today waters many towns along its lower reaches. The Chu River no longer issues from the Issyk-kul'; it flows near the lake shore. Archaeologists have attributed this shift to the alluvial flow in the T'ien-shan area.

Hsüan-tsang, in his *Great T'ang Chronicle of the Western Marches*, refers to the Issyk-kul' by such names as "the steaming sea," "the briny sea," and "the great clear pond"—doubtless because the lake never freezes and its water, though salty, is pellucid. An analysis of its salt content, a Russian archaeologist has written, shows that the lake may be a hundred thousand years old. The question is: should we believe this scientific calculation, or should we believe the ancient tradition of the people who live on its shores? The choice should doubtless be left to the reader.

Princess Yung-t'ai's Necklace

Translated by
Edward Seidensticker

It was in the year 907 that the T'ang Dynasty came to an end, twenty reigns and two hundred ninety years after its founding; and that Chu Ch'üan-chung, seizing power from the last of the T'ang, ascended the throne and proclaimed the founding of the Liang Dynasty. There followed a half century of civil wars. Five successive conquerors sought to found dynasties, taking for themselves the dynastic names Liang, T'ang, Chin, Han, and Chou. They came and went in a dizzying succession.

Historical records inform us that in the period of the Five Dynasties most of the royal T'ang tombs were entered and robbed. Ch'ang-an and Lo-yang, the T'ang capitals, were laid waste by repeated battles and abandoned, and the center of political power moved far to the north. Doubtless there was no one to notice when tombs near the two cities were pillaged. Tombs of the old aristocracy were especially numerous in the environs of Ch'ang-an. Soon after it crosses the Wei River the road westwards from Ch'ang-an divides, one fork leading to Kansu Province and the other to Szechwan. Beyond the fork, Han and T'ang tombs dot the plain in large numbers. All are domes of earth, some as large as small mountains, some no more than mounds. There are royal tombs and tombs of warriors, and tombs of no one knows whom. It is recorded that so eminent a person as Wên Yün, a grand marshal in the age of the Five Dynasties, opened T'ang tombs in large numbers, and so it seems most likely that tomb robbing, while it may have been a somewhat gloomy and dangerous pursuit, offered powerful inducements to the ordinary ruffians of the time. The "seven implements" of the robber-excavators, at the sophistication of which modern archaeologists have expressed astonished admiration, were probably developed in the vicinity of Ch'ang-an and Lo-yang in the period of the Five Dynasties.

It is probably correct to say that the robbery of the tomb of Princess Yung-t'ai, here to be described, occurred at about this time. The tomb is at the foot of the heights known as Liang-shan, near the town of Ch'ien-hsien in Shensi Province; in a more general sense it may be thought of as at the north-west corner of the great plain of the tombs, to the west of Ch'ang-an, where waves of hills begin to rise beyond the plain that has stretched like a board from Ch'ang-an. On the highest of them is the grand tomb of the T'ang Emperor Kao Tsung and Empress Wu. Princess Yung-t'ai's tomb lies on the southeast flank of the grand tomb.

It would be good if I could here record the precise date of the robbing of the princess's tomb. Unfortunately there remains no clue in our search for a date. "On a certain night in a certain year in the unsettled times of the Five Dynasties, about a thousand years ago": there seems no other way to begin our story.

༄

Ch'en, the head of the robber band, did not know who was buried in the funeral mound upon which he had set his eye. He made casual inquiry among the elders of the village, but no one was in possession of the knowledge. It did not especially stand out among the mounds that dotted the plain. It was among the larger ones, but it was not remarkably large even so.

Among the tombs in the region, only the grand tomb was clearly identified. Everyone knew that Kao Tsung and Empress

Wu of the T'ang lay buried there. The funeral mountain is visible from the farthest reaches of the plain. As one approaches from Ch'ang-an, two independent mountains are sighted. At the summits are strange protuberances, like fragments of a castle wall. They are the portals guarding the grand tomb, but the villagers have long called them "The Breasts of Empress Wu." From a distance they do indeed look like breasts, the protuberances forming the nipples. As one approaches, a third mountain comes into view beyond the others. It contains the royal tombs. From the plain the three look like independent hills, but ascending an elevation one sees that they are three eminences rising from a single mountain.

Only the grand tomb has been clearly identified, and only it has escaped the robbers. It is not known where inside the mountain the emperor and empress rest. Even if the general site of the funeral crypts might be surmised, a digging would be more than a band of a hundred or two hundred could manage. It would doubtless be necessary for some thousands of coolies to labor for months on end, and virtually level the mountain.

Ch'ên had many times climbed to the top of the grand tomb. He knew that it was beyond his capabilities, and yet his footsteps would lead him to it, and he would ask if there might not somewhere be a beginning. In ancient times there doubtless was a funeral road from "The Breasts" to the tombs. Today the whole of the way is knee-deep in weeds and creepers, and broken stone figures of men and animals give uncertain evidence that there once was a road. There is no tombstone. The tomb is the whole of a natural mountain, and somewhere deep inside it are two sarcophagi in which lie emperor and empress. As he came to "The Breasts," Ch'ên would find his thoughts running wild.

His climbs were not wholly without purpose. From the summit he would study the plain, and on one of his climbs in the spring it came to him that the mound flanking the grand tomb was somehow different from the tens of others dotting the plain. Ch'ên almost cried out in this new awareness: was not the mound here below him somehow attached to and attendant upon the grand tomb? He was more and more certain. It was not likely that a tomb of such magnitude would be without an auxiliary, and if indeed there was such a tomb, then its position suggested strongly that the one which he now looked down upon, flanking the grand tomb, would be it.

Eyes aglow, he scanned the plain once more. It seemed to him that the grand tomb suddenly pushed forth and spread its skirts yet farther over the plain. He wanted another mound to balance the first, and give symmetry to the grand tomb. But there was no such mound.

He could not all the same rid himself of the notion that the mound which had attracted his attention was auxiliary to the grand tomb. If indeed it was, then royalty or high nobility must lie buried there. Suddenly the mound seemed to glow with a strange light. It was covered with weeds, and even the fabric woven by the weeds seemed soft and elegant, somehow different and significant. The hope and the excitement known only to a robber of tombs as he opens a sarcophagus—once more it came flooding over him. Treasures, still and quiet in ancient, stagnant air! A necklace of jasper, a sword inlaid with gold!

Descending to the plain, he skirted the grand tomb and approached the mound that had caught his eye. A road not far away might be troublesome when work was commenced, but the land lay deep in weeds, as if no one had ventured in for many years.

Tirelessly he walked about. He came upon a cubical stone buried some twenty yards from the mound. Perhaps there had once been a paving of such stones, and only this one remained. He thought the shape of the mound most pleasing. Nothing now disturbed the roundness at the top, but it seemed to him that there had once been a sort of constriction, as of an inverted bowl. He kicked at the the mound and took up dirt in his hands, and walked around the base again and again, and climbed to the top. Then he started back across the flats from what he took to be the front of the tomb. He walked slowly as if something were holding him back.

On his face was the savage expression it always wore when he had decided to open a tomb. The line of the jaw was firm, the eyes were fixed and unmoving. It could be done, he thought. There was no evidence that anyone had dug before him. If the mound was indeed in attendance upon the grand tomb, then it would contain great treasures. The digging would probably take ten men a week. Even in an age of civil disturbance grave robbing was a capital offense. The work must be done in the few hours of deepest night.

But Ch'ên was not afraid. It was at the age of sixteen that he had first helped open a tomb, and now, at forty, he could not have said how many tombs he had been in. Not once had he made a mistake. His fellows said that when Ch'ên set his eyes on a grave, the sarcophagus would come floating agreeably up from the depths of the earth and put itself at his disposal. It was his way to do a thing immediately when he had put his mind to it. He thought that he would assemble a band tonight, even, for consultations. They would begin work in the dark, moonless nights. The tomb was fortunately a half day's journey from Ch'ang-an. The season was such that even in the daytime passers-by were few. There were five or six villages nearby, and life in them was at the lowest subsistence level. The young men had all been conscripted, and only the old and women and children remained. Ch'ên himself was from one of the villages. He had long lived in Ch'ang-an, but because of the unrest of these last years he was more often to be seen in his native village than in the city.

His fellows were always ready. In each of the villages there were men with whom he had worked over the years. Most of them were old, but they were experienced and reliable.

Unlike the young, they did not talk. In whatever straits they might find themselves they did not kill and they robbed only graves. To rob a grave was of course to rob, but somehow they did not think of the work as thievery. What was wrong, they asked, with digging up an ownerless something from the earth? There was a strange defiance in the question. But though they did not complain, the opening of graves was not pleasant work. There was a certain darkness of countenance about a grave robber that was recognized by others in the fellowship. As if by agreement, they spoke in low tones, and did not often laugh.

Three nights were required to open a shaft. Most commonly the main funeral passage lay directly below the earthen mound, and the crypt itself, containing the sarcophagus, lay at some remove. Sometimes, to confuse robbers, the main passage, the inner passage, and the crypt itself bore no relation at all to the external mound. The several cuts would wind and twist, and then the door to the crypt would be at the spot least expected. Sometimes it was by no means easy even to find the crypt. Incomparably more difficult was the task of getting the funeral treasures out. These were of course the tombs of the rich and noble. They had been devised on the assumption that there would be robbers.

The first stroke of the mattock determined whether the work would proceed smoothly or with very great difficulty. Ko, a bent old man of seventy, was the recognized expert. On this first night he was the busy one. He would throw himself down on the ground tens and scores of times. He would lie face down here and there, his ear pressed to the mound, as if listening for voices within. For the others, there was something heartening and something very mysterious about Ko's face in the lamplight. He would open his eyes and close them and open them again.

"This will be the way inside."

At these words from Ko, a stir would pass through the company. Seven or eight times out of ten Ko would be right. If they dug where he told them to dig, they would generally come upon one or another of the passages, deep below the ground.

This time, after repeated tests, Ko lay down at a spot to the northeast. He turned and turned, now with his left ear and now with his right to the mound.

"Try digging here," he finally said. "I don't know how far down, but there's an opening. This is one of the easy ones."

What he meant was that there were apparently no special devices for misleading robbers. Late each night the band would go off to the tomb. For three nights the ten of them took turns at digging. Some forty feet below the spot chosen by Ko they came upon a flat rock about a yard square which might have been called a skylight. It was deeper than they would have expected, but in the sense that it led directly in from the skirt of the mound, the tomb was perhaps "one of the easy ones." The stone was too large for two or three men to move. Since they were confined to the narrow shaft they had opened, they were two nights making their way into the passage below. When finally they had succeeded, there was still a little time before daybreak. Some in the band wanted to proceed immediately, but Ch'ên said with some firmness that they would wait until the next night. Against possible discovery, they had yet to block the shaft and cover it with weeds. The secret of grave robbing was to leave time for everything.

It was a cloudy night of fierce winds when they finally made their way inside. The band seemed to gather from nowhere, work clothes beating in the wind. The season was neither warm nor cold. The light of the lanterns was now bright, now low.

Ch'ên looked from one to another. They were not to have thoughts of private booty, he said, They were to share alike. And he approached a young woman, the only woman among them, and a tall young man.

"You two will stand guard outside," he said.

The woman was his third wife, the man his younger brother.

"Get inside, the rest of you."

As if in a sort of ceremonial capacity as leader, he took up a lantern and bent over to enter the dark hole. Three men followed him and mattocks and shovels and hammers and the like were brought down, and the other four disappeared inside.

The darkness was more profound than on the surface. The only sound was the whistling of the wind. He had left as sentinels his wife and a brother with whom he shared the same blood, and in the choice had been considerations of a sort that Ch'ên would make. Had he chosen anyone else, he could not have been sure when the stone would be toppled back into place. The others were his trusted comrades, but they were human, and he could not be sure when temptation would raise its head. If the stone were to fall, if only that were to happen, then the men inside would not see the light of day again. Ten days would pass and they would lie dead of starvation, and the treasure would be the property of him who had betrayed them. The men in the tomb were always conscious, therefore, of who it was that stood watch outside. Though it was the usual thing for a relative of someone inside the tomb to be drafted for the work, that was not always the safest procedure. There were wives who cursed husbands, sons who hated fathers. Ch'ên's choice of his own wife and brother had much to recommend it to the others. Ch'ên's young wife got along well with her husband, and she was a good-natured, amiable woman, pleasant to everyone. The brother had been reared like a son. He was of a wholesome nature such as to deny that he and Ch'ên shared the same blood, and well thought of by everyone.

But it was not as wise a choice as the others thought it. The moment the two were alone the woman held out her hand to the man.

"Put the lid back on. Make up your mind to it. Go in and do it."

She spoke in a low voice. The young man was startled. The same terrible thought had been with him from the moment he was appointed sentinel. He had been having an affair with the woman for a year and more. Though she was his brother's wife she did not seem like a sister-in-law. Ch'ên had taken advantage of the fact that she was without resources, and had as good as kidnapped her, and had his way with her.

There was a rustling as the youth went off through the grass. The woman followed.

"Do it," she whispered again.

Her thin body was trembling, perhaps from the horror of the words. She trembled, and there was hot urgency in them. Ch'ên had not yet guessed what was happening, she said, but he would, sooner or later. They would do well to ask themselves what would happen when he did. They would be the ones to end up in a grave. They could not guess what shape the murders would take. He was still young, she said. He could make a good living for himself without robbing graves. She was from the countryside beyond the Yellow River, where people lived in peace and quiet. Why not cross over, the two of them, and make a happy life for themselves? It would be a pity, of course, to shut up all those old men in the tomb; but they had done bad things in their time, and they did not have much life ahead of them in any event. They would be dead in a few years whatever happened. It would only mean putting them in a tomb two or three years early.

The youth was thinking of something else. His brother was a born rogue who had done many bad things. The youth himself had been among the victims. But he had come thus far because he had a brother. Still, it was as the woman said: the two of them would one day be cut down. They could not rest while Ch'ên lived. The youth knew that he was trembling even more violently than she. He walked off. She was at his side, her body pressed to his. Still the wind blew across the plain.

"I'll go have a look," said the youth, when they had come to the shaft.

He said only that, and stooped to go down inside. She held her breath—because she thought that he was about to do as she had suggested? There were footholds along the shaft. The young man went down from one to the next. When his hand touched the great stone that had been raised to open the passage he recoiled. A chill swept over him.

Below it hung a rope ladder, the only way down into the passage. He climbed yet further inside. He was himself once more. He had abandoned his sentinel duties and come inside because the horror there on the surface had been too much for him. The temptation to push the great stone over did not leave him. It would be the work of an instant, and require only a very little strength.

Here inside the tomb it was cold as ice. He could hear a chipping of stone. It was a dark, forbidding sound. He groped his way toward it. There was water on the ground, so cold that his feet were soon numb. Presently there was a dim light. There were lanterns along both walls of the passage, to make it somewhat more like a place of work. The robbers stood in a cluster. They looked around at his approach.

"Don't scare us," said one of them.

Ch'ên too turned an apprehensive look upon him, but said nothing. There was a stepladder, on which one of the robbers stood as he wielded a large mallet. The youth saw now that the shaft was blocked by a stone door. The crypt would be inside.

"Let me have a swing at it. I'm freezing."

Another man mounted the ladder. He called out, keeping time to the swinging of the mallet. The door was a strong one.

Though chips of stone flew through the air, it showed no sign of giving. The men took turn after turn on the ladder. They were like blue and red devils at work in an inferno.

"You have a try at it," said Ch'ên abruptly to his brother.

The youth mounted the ladder. He had to do something, he thought, to keep from freezing. He took up the largest of the mallets. Did he expect to use that oversized sledge, someone said. Leaning forward, he swung it in a wide sweep and came down upon it with all his strength. At a great rending he was thrown from the ladder and left sitting in a pool of water.

When he was on his feet again his eight fellows were already disappearing through a hole at the top of the door. They took lanterns with them. The shaft was soon in darkness. He took up a lantern and climbed into the crypt. It was a narrow rectangular space, somewhat brighter because of the narrowness.

It's just a hallway, muttered someone. The room next door, said another. A damned nuisance, said a third. It did indeed seem to be the case that the sarcophagus lay in the room beyond. The tomb had both vestibule and crypt.

"Bring me a light," called Ch'ên. He was looking at a square stone in the middle of the vestibule, on which was inscribed the history of the tomb.

"You can read," said Ch'ên to his brother. "What does it say?"

They were all looking at the stone, but the youth was the only one who could read.

"Princess Yung-t'ai, born Li Hsien-hui. Seventh daughter of T'ang Chung Tsung."

These were the first words. He read for his brother.

"In 700 she was enfiefed as a princess of the first rank. She was married to Wu Yen-chi, King of Wei, and died at the age of seventeen.

"First buried on the outskirts of Ch'ang-an, she was reinterred in 706 upon the death of the Empress Wu and the reaccession of Chung Tsung. She rests in this tomb, auxiliary to the grand tomb."

The youth was not able to read the whole of the inscription. There were passages which he could read and passages which he could not.

"I don't get it all," muttered Ch'ên, as if satisfied. "It belongs with the grand tomb. That much is clear. Let's get at it."

He felt at the door beyond. It looked easy, he said. A blow or two would do it.

"We'll have a try at it tomorrow. We'll work all tomorrow night, and get everything out."

No one dissented. What they wanted most was to get outside and warm up a bit. Their teeth were chattering violently. They went out through the same hole and as good as raced one another up the rope ladder.

Ch'ên called to the woman. There was a rustling in the darkness, and she arose from a clump of grass. Eyes averted, the youth followed at a short distance. Perhaps the wind had died down—there was not in any event the shrill whistling of earlier. The woman waited for him to come up.

"No good." That was all she said.

"Have you heard of Princess Yung-t'ai?" He wanted to change the subject.

"The one who said bad things about Empress Wu and was killed?"

The youth remembered now. He had heard the story as a child. The empress would be the one in the grand tomb, familiar to everyone hereabouts because of "The Breasts."

The story he had heard was that the princess, granddaughter of the empress, incurred the empress's displeasure because of certain unfriendly remarks, and, with her husband, was whipped to death. The story had to do less with the tragic princess than with the extraordinary nature of the empress, stronger and more self-willed than any man. It had frightened him as a child. And now they were robbing the tomb where the unfortunate T'ang princess slept. The work seemed intolerably distasteful.

He followed the woman. Her footsteps were like a board slapping the earth. He was thinking that there had been more unfortunate women than she now walking the plain in the dawn with the robber band.

✿

In the evening twilight the next day, the robber band gathered before the tomb of Princess Yung-t'ai. There was not the wind of last night, but it was raining. Showers from morning had become a steady fall. The robbers had bundled themselves against the underground cold, and they wore rain capes as well.

They were identical bundles of clothing. In the dim lamplight it was not possible to tell one from another.

"You stand watch," said Ch'ên to the woman.

Tonight there would be only one sentinel. Ahead lay the work of bringing treasures from the storehouse. It would not do to have even one man idle.

Ch'ên went down first. Ko followed. Ko reached for a foothold with his left leg, which always hurt when it rained, and was slow and awkward as he climbed inside. The vigor and vitality with which he had scented out hollows in the tomb were quite gone.

The young man went in last. As he bent to go inside he heard the woman's voice.

"No good."

She seemed to have given up hope of inciting him to action. Her voice was a mingling of resignation and despair. And then she whispered that she would go to him the next night. If they were caught—well, they would think what to do after they had been caught.

PRINCESS YUNG-T'AI'S NECKLACE

The youth went down in silence. Rain had washed at the footholds. He could easily have slipped and fallen to the subterranean floor.

There were twice as many lanterns as the night before. He had been able to make out little, but tonight the details were fairly clear. It was more than just an underground shaft. As befitted the tomb of an aristocrat, the floor was paved with bricks, and the walls were covered with paintings. There were six openings above and four niches along each wall. Ko had detected one of the six. The robbers had made their cut and come through it. In one direction the passage led to the crypts. In the other it probably led to an outer passage, but short of that it was already lost in darkness.

The youth approached one of the niches. It was stuffed with ceramic figures in large numbers. There were standing human figures in decorated porcelain, and horsemen, and horses with tricolor glazes, and there was a confusion of utensils and saucers that doubtless had been for everyday use. Some had fallen from the niche and lay on the floor. These were playthings, however, that did not interest the robbers. They were probably offerings with which the princess's intimates had shown their sympathy.

Suddenly a great rending of the brick wall shook the ancient air. Starting from his reverie, the youth climbed through the hole he himself had opened the night before.

The vestibule was bright with the light of several lanterns. The robbers were not to be seen. There was a large hole in the door to the inner crypt, and fragments of brick lay scattered about. The youth went into the crypt, where lay the sarcophagus.

He pulled back in astonishment. There was a large stone sarcophagus and there were murals on all the walls. He had followed his brother into countless graves, but he had not seen one so beautifully decorated.

The robbers were lost in their appraisal of the funeral objects on the floor. Most were in boxes, which however had decayed, so that it was no problem to descry the contents.

The youth did a turn around the sarcophagus, looking at the murals. Ch'ên and the others were already hard at work, and there was no one to reprove him. He had a leisurely look at the paintings. Everywhere were clusters of court ladies and serving women. He stood somewhat longer before the east wall. There was a red pillar at the center. To the left were seven ladies and to the right nine, all of them with this and that object in their hands. He wondered if they might have served Princess Yung-t'ai. In one of the figures he could see the profile of the woman who stood guard in the rainy night.

He looked up. There was something on the ceiling too. The light was too dim to permit detailed examination, but he could see a scattering of stars, and the moon and the sun, and crows and rabbits and the like. A night sky, he said to himself. On the great sarcophagus there were line incisions of people and flowers and birds and animals.

"Up here, you. Let's get the lid off."

It was Ch'ên's voice above him. Legs wide apart, Ch'ên was standing on the sarcophagus and waving hands in large gloves. The youth did not know why he should be waving so energetically, but that he was very excited was clear. Another of the robbers climbed up, and a second. Others were at work on the lid, pushing from the four sides. It resisted even a lever.

"What do you think you're up to? Sightseeing?" he shouted at the youth.

The youth joined the others. The heavy lid finally slipped a foot or so.

Ch'ên held a lantern to the opening.

"There's a necklace," he growled, in thick, heavy tones. "You. Get inside."

This last he said to a man on the stone beside him.

"Not me." The refusal was plain and firm.

Ch'ên called off the names of the other men. Not one of them said that he would. This hesitation was not in their nature.

"Give it up," said Ko. "It's more important to get these things outside. And we have to get them home. It will be morning."

They would have to hurry, said another. The carts would get stuck in the mud, said a third. There were other comments. And indeed the robbers had collected large numbers of funeral objects and piled them in heaps. Among them was an urn which a man could barely have encircled with his arms, and a coffer containing no one could have said what. There was a table, there were pots, many of them. They lay scattered about the crypt.

Still not satisfied, Ch'ên held his lantern to the opening time after time. The youth looked at him, and hated him. For the first time he hated this brother whose blood he shared—hated him intensely.

Ch'ên climbed from the sarcophagus, and they began the work of carrying their booty outside. They went back and forth, crypt to vestibule to passage and back again, their arms loaded. No one felt the cold as they had felt it the night before. Presently they commenced carrying things from the passage to the surface. In the second process was a kind of confirmation. It signified that what they had was theirs.

They climbed to the surface and down and up again, three and four times. Even so the number of objects ranged on the ground seemed insignificant.

"We aren't getting very far," said Ch'ên, ordering a short rest. They sat down among the pools in the shaft. Just then the woman called down.

"I hear horses neighing. And not just ten or twenty of them, either."

Ch'ên jumped up and reached for the ladder.

"Which way?"

"The east, and the west too."

"What do you think it means?"

"I don't know. A battle maybe. I can hear them in the north now, and in the south too."

The robber band had gathered at the opening.

"Come on out. We'll be better off away from here. There's probably still time."

"She's right," said Ch'ên. "Put the lights out and go on up, and scatter once you've covered the hole." He gave the command briskly.

The robbers returned to the crypt and took lanterns from the walls, extinguishing them as if by command as they gathered once more at the rope ladder. They climbed one by one from the passage, now in pitch darkness.

The youth was the last to emerge. He looked at the faces of his comrades and saw that Ch'ên was not among them. He could indeed hear a neighing of cavalry horses. They were not far away. Troops seemed to be massing out over the plain. It was raining harder.

He went down inside once more. He went to the aperture. The passage was in darkness. He waited for his brother, who would be in the crypt. What would he be doing?

A faint light appeared at the end of the passage. It grew brighter, and the youth made out the figure of his brother. Light in hand, Ch'ên looked up.

"Who's that? Let's get out of here."

The youth did not answer.

The lantern lighted about a third of the passage. Ch'ên seemed to be looking at something in his hand. Then he reached for the ladder.

The youth saw that he had a necklace in his hand; and as he saw it the earlier revulsion came over him once more. It changed to anger, an anger that would not relent, not even upon the command of the heavens. Ch'ên had gone inside the sarcophagus! With his dirty feet he had intruded upon the sleep of the unhappy young princess! He had stolen her necklace!

Scarcely knowing what he did, the youth laid his hand upon the stone. Without so great a noise it fell and covered the passage. It closed the aperture completely, like a lid fashioned by a master craftsman. Slowly the youth climbed to the surface. The rest of the band had disappeared. So they had all run away, he said to himself. The woman came up to him. Silently, whether or not she knew what he had done, she took up a large shovel and started filling the hole. It was then that they began to hear arrows in the driving rain.

※

In August, 1960, the tomb of Princess Yung-t'ai was excavated by archaeologists of the Cultural Properties Commission of Shensi Privince.

The tomb had been robbed, but more than a thousand funeral objects yet remained. A skeleton, probably of one of the robbers, was found inside the opening through which the robbers had entered, and funeral jewels were scattered around it.

Aside from the funeral objects, the most important find was the murals. That on the west wall of the passage had flaked badly, but that on the east was in relatively good condition. The murals on the four walls of the inner crypt had also deteriorated badly, only that on the east still retaining something of its original form.

In line and color, in form and treatment of space, the murals are of a very high order, important materials in the history of T'ang painting. The damage to the paintings, said one of the archaeologists, was caused by rain and dampness from the hole opened by the robbers. The passage and the crypts, he said, were deep in refuse.

Along with her husband Wu Yen-chi and her brother, Chung-hun, King of Shao, Princess Yung-t'ai incurred the displeasure of Empress Wu and was put to death. After the accession of her father, Chung Tsung, all three were rehabilitated, and moved from their original graves outside Ch'ang-an to the foot of Liang-shan. There is no other example before or since, it is said, of designating a princess's grave a grand tomb; and so one may imagine the sorrow of Chung Tsung for his daughter.

The Opaline Cup

Translated by
James T. Araki

I have known Kuwashima Tatsuya, a professor of archaeology in Kyoto, for many years. I mentioned in a recent
letter that I hoped to visit Kyoto for the autumn leaves—
something I had not done in years. I had quite forgotten
my letter when I received this reply, scribbled on a postcard:
"A cut-glass piece, originally from the tomb of Emperor
Ankan, has turned up recently in Fusé. It's known as the
Opaline Cup. Once it goes into someone's private collection
it might disappear for good. If you're coming anyway, why
not come in time to see it? You'll have to get here before
the month is out. Autumn will soon be over, you know."
It was just like Kuwashima, a man wholly absorbed in his
work as an archaeologist, to assume that others would be
just as fascinated with archaeological findings.

There was a time during my university days when
Kuwashima had me interested in ancient objects, but I must
confess that old vases, teacups, and such are now far removed
from my concerns. Still, the resolute message from Kuwashima
aroused my curiosity. Though I knew nothing at all about the
ancient piece, I thought I should take the opportunity to see it.
Besides, there was some truth in what I had written, about
wanting to see the autumn foliage, and I had thought of taking
a vacation before the cold set in. I decided to accede to
Kuwashima's urgings and, with them as my chief reason,

make a trip to Kyoto, where I had spent my three years as a university student.

My fascination with the cup was due not so much to its rarity as the fact that it had belonged to Emperor Ankan. I once had reason to become familiar with the names of Emperor Ankan and Princess Kasuga, two among the countless ones mentioned in the ancient chronicles, and I have not forgotten them. An article that had been placed in Ankan's tomb must be something the emperor treasured, perhaps used regularly. My interest in the cup was not centered on anything as specific as its historical significance or its value as an art object. I was attracted to it because of its association with that particular sovereign.

🌢

Kizu Motosuké, my brother-in-law, was the one who had etched the names of Emperor Ankan and Princess Kasuga in my mind, ten years before.

I became acquainted with Kizu when we were classmates in middle school. He shared my interest in literature and that was the reason, I suppose, why I got along with him best and regarded him as my closest friend. After we went on to different high schools we did not see each other quite as often. He eventually graduated from a private university and began to teach at a middle school for girls. I came to think of him as a good match for my younger sister, Tao.

Though Kizu was on the somber side, he tended to be deliberate in whatever he did, and I admired the trait. I thought he would make an ideal husband for Tao, whose chief recommendation was her docility. Kizu had been a frequent visitor to our house when we were classmates, and he and Tao had come to know each other rather well. I had been responsible for Tao since our parents' death, and I worried about her. In the end, despite whatever misgivings I might have had about seeing her married at such a young age, just out of middle school, I arranged to have Kizu marry her.

Much to my surprise Kizu and Tao did not seem happy together. Tao died five years later. I think I can count the few occasions when Tao's face was lit with carefree laughter during those years. It is difficult to say which of the two was responsible, but Kizu at least seemed to recognize some obscure, deep-set reason for their incompatibility.

Tao had given wholly of herself to Kizu. Because she expected as much in return, she was inevitably disappointed and discontented. She tried to gain Kizu's affection through a touching display of devotion, and I can remember how sorry I felt for her.

Tao often complained about Kizu's coolness. I thought it unwise to bare her complaints and make an issue of a discord that lay concealed beneath the calm facade of their marriage. And so I would try to comfort her. Kizu had not changed; he had always been a chilly sort. I was not inclined to be patient with Tao, even though I was the only one to whom she could turn, and I did not trouble myself to discuss all her complaints with her. Tao's death left me burdened with a sense of guilt. Whenever I think of her, even now, more than ten years later, I feel the sharp sting of self-reproach.

It was toward the end of spring, as I recall, a month or so after Tao died, that I went to see Kizu, who was living alone in a house suddenly untidy and cheerless.

Kizu had just got home from work. He had not bothered to change and was sitting beside a table on the veranda, leaning on an elbow. Apparently unaware that I had walked in, he sat there in the gathering dusk, staring vacantly out at the little garden. When I spoke he turned and answered. I was startled by the dark melancholy that overspread his face.

I do not recall why I went to see him. I do recall, however, that I tried not to mention Tao, for the wounds were not yet healed.

Soon we were drinking, and for some reason began talking about an episode in *The Chronicle of Japan*. Kizu took down from the shelves a bulky volume, an annotated edition of *The Chronicle*, and put it before me with the pages opened. He prevailed upon me to read a poem by Crown Prince Ankan that spoke of his love for Princess Kasuga, newly become his consort, and the princess's reply. The poems are introduced thus: "They held sweet converse all through the moonlit night till the dawn came upon them unawares. The courtly elegance of verse was suddenly embodied in his speech, and he broke into song. . . ."

I was familiar with Ankan's poem, which I had first heard in a university lecture. I recalled having been much moved. It begins:

> Throughout the eight islands
> Vainly did I seek a wife.
> Then I was told:
> In Kasuga, land of the spring sun,
> There lives a fair maiden,
> I was told
> There lives a good maiden. . . .

I remembered clearly that my young senses were aroused by the vivid description of physical intimacy:

> Her arm was around me,
> And my arm too was around her. . . .

But I had no recollection of Princess Kasuga's reply. I learned from Kizu that the princess's poem was actually an elegy she composed when the emperor died, and that for some strange reason it had been entered at this point in the narrative.

"It's an elegy she composed at his funeral," Kizu said. "That's the accepted theory. But, that aside, what do you make of it?"

He spoke rather abruptly, in the manner of a much older man which he often affected. He looked intently at the text he had put before me, and then began reciting in an odd singsong style:

Down the river of Hatsusé
Hidden amid mountains,
A bamboo comes floating—
A goodly stalk with tender branches;
From its lower part I fashion a koto,
From its upper part I fashion a flute,
And I sound them.
I ascend to the top of Mimuro,
Where I stand and scan the land below.
The fishes in the water
Of the pond of Ihare of creeping vines
Would come to the surface and lament.
The sash of fine and comely weave
Once worn by our great sovereign
Whose reign brought peace to the land
Now hangs loose.
No man is there
But would raise his voice in lament.

This doubtless was the way he recited poetry in the class-room. It was almost funny, and yet there was a strange ring of sadness to the off-key melody.

When he had finished the recitation, in all seriousness he said: "Do you understand what it means? Such a sad poem! It must be sad, of course. It's a dirge after all. It's a sad poem, a very sad poem. But, then, it makes me wonder whether Princess Kasuga actually loved the emperor. Her sadness is expressed much too neatly. It seems unrelated to love. It seems more a rejection of love. I don't see her grieving at all. She notices everything and everybody lamenting his death, and she speaks for them. She might not have loved the emperor. But when he died she must have been sad, terribly sad. It's the kind of sadness I can understand."

Kizu talked on as if possessed. At first I thought there must be something wrong with him, but he seemed to be quite in possession of himself. I could tell, however, that he was overcome by violent emotions. I was accustomed to his ardor and decisiveness on subjects that moved him, but never before had he been so eloquent and emotional, or spoken to me at such length, looking me straight in the eye, unsmiling.

Uneasily I sipped at my wine, not interrupting him. Kizu continued, more or less repeating himself: "Here we have side by side two poems that are very different. Love pulses through Emperor Ankan's poem. It's genuine. How he must have loved her! But the princess has all her wits about her. No one truly in love could come up with a poem like hers. And yet she must have been sad. Of course she was sad."

It finally came to me that perhaps Kizu was making a confession. Every word now seemed like an apology for his unkindness to Tao, my sister. And there was self-pity! Suddenly it all seemed very distasteful. When he began again reciting, softly, in that odd singsong style, I shouted that I had had enough.

I was aware of the ring of cruelty in my voice. Kizu fell silent and started drinking, for there was not much else to do now, and was soon drunk from the little wine he had had. He fell as he stepped down from the veranda for a drink of water. He pushed himself from the ground, quite without dignity. As he walked unsteadily toward the well, he looked far older than his years, and lonely. I knew that something was very wrong. The way he had fallen, and pushed himself wearily up, and staggered to the well—suggested not so much drunkenness as the hollow shell of a man.

Kizu Motosuké was recruited into the army and died three years later in a hospital in North China. I have no way of knowing how he had felt on that night, but I have twinges of regret whenever I recall my obduracy. Kizu evidently had not been pretending. His words and acts suggested that the death of his young wife had hurt him grievously—a wife for whom he had felt very little affection. I was sure that he had tried very honestly to communicate his sorrow.

Whenever I think of my sister's short, unhappy life, or of Kizu, I think of those words, "Down the river of Hatsusé, hidden amid mountains . . . ," and just as unfailingly Kizu's peculiar singsong recitation. I have never bothered to check his interpretation of the poem, but I have come to feel rather fond of that ancient monarch, a tragic man, very human, quite unlike the other godly figures of antiquity.

So I answered Kuwashima Tatsuya's invitation to see the cut-glass cup. Doubtless my interest was aroused by the fact that it had belonged to the monarch at whose funeral had sounded that strange, sad dirge.

♥

I arrived in Kyoto the end of November, barely within the time limit set by Kuwashima. Though it was near dusk and perhaps too late to find Kuwashima still in his office, I went straight from the station to the university. The campus was already in the shadows of evening.

Kuwashima was just getting ready to leave. "You barely caught me," he said, dispensing with the customary greetings.

"You might have sent me a wire to let me know you were coming." We hadn't seen each other in three years, and he was obviously delighted.

We sat down in a narrow space in a corner of his office, which was cluttered with display cases. Artifacts crowded the shelves and tables.

"So this is your office," I said, looking around.

"How many years do you think it's been since I got my B.A.? Isn't it about time I had a room or two of my own?" He laughed heartily as if struck by the humor in his own remark, which could be interpreted as either self-congratulation or diffidence.

He switched on the light. In the suddenly bright room dark shadows outlined the many oddly shaped objects. There in a crevice of light I saw Kuwashima's boyish face, now etched more deeply with the weariness of old age but, as before, reflecting the calm of a man who is dedicated to his work and has no other cares.

"Can I still see it?" I asked.

"Oh, the cup from Ankan's tomb. Can you see it? You don't know how lucky you are." He beamed as if to share what he presumed to be my delight, and told me that someone just a few days before had come up with the fascinating idea of placing the cup side by side with the glass cup that had been stored in the Shōsō-in since the eighth century.

Kuwashima then proceeded to tell me, with his customary eloquence, about Emperor Ankan's cup.

I learned that anyone who has ever studied archaeology is familiar with this cut-glass piece and its name, the Opaline Cup, because it is so named in documents of the Edo Period. But the cup itself had been lost until it was rediscovered in Fusé. "The nature of the stone of which it is made is not known," one document states. The mystery has been solved; we now know that it is glass.

The entry on the Sairin-ji in Furuichi County in *The Illustrated Guide to Famous Sites in Kawachi*, published in 1801, contains this description: "The Opaline Cup is a treasure of the monastery. It is four-and-a-half inches in diameter and three inches high. The exterior and base are decorated, star-like, with series of circular designs. The nature of the stone of which it is made is not known. It is said to have been among the many articles that were exposed when the bank of Emperor Ankan's tomb disintegrated during a flood some eighty years ago. The cup was found on the property of a farmer named Tanaka of Sonnai. He donated it to this monastery."

Miura Ranhan's *A Few Facts on Ancient Kawachi*, published in 1804, also states that the Opaline Cup emerged from the bank of Emperor Ankan's tomb. Quite evidently the treasured cup of the Sairin-ji was well known at the time.

Ōta Nampo, better known as the comic poet Shokusanjin, recorded in his *Tales and Words* the writings of Kuzu Keirai and the Kyoto tea master Sōtatsu; he grouped them under the heading of "Records of the Opaline Cup of Furuichi in Kawachi Province." Fujii Teikan's *Collection of Ancient Paintings* has a sketch of the cup.

Kuzu says in his essay in *Tales and Words*: "After the wars, villagers broke into the sacred tomb. A servant of the village headman Kamiya excavated the Opaline Cup. It was retained by the Kamiya family for more than a hundred years, and then was presented as an offering to the Sairin-ji." Kuzu's essay was written in 1796. The actual find was made in the late seventeenth century, during the Genroku Era.

The cup, then, had either been removed from Ankan's tomb or unearthed accidentally by a flood during Genroku, kept in the Kamiya family for a century or more, and brought to the Sairin-ji and become a well-known treasure. When the Meiji Government adopted the policy of debasing Buddhism and destroying Buddhist idols, however, the many buildings of the Sairin-ji fell into neglect and eventually disappeared. The cup and all other treasures of the monastery vanished.

"The cup is itself an extraordinary find," Kuwashima said. "But what fascinates us more is that it seems to match the glass cup in the Shōsō-in. If this is so, it's bound to raise some interesting questions."

The items in the Shōsō-in, according to Kuwashima, date from the reign of Emperor Shōmu in the eighth century. If the cup that had belonged to Shōmu matched the cup from Ankan's tomb, it must be just as old—and so its dating would have to be revised.

"The only plausible conclusion we can reach," Kuwashima explained to me, "is that the two glass cups were made in the same era, and by the same artisan. They're alike in shape, size, even the cut design. They say the cup in the Shōsō-in was brought to Japan from Persia by way of China and Korea.

I'm sure it was the same with the other cup. I can't say until I see them side by side, but they must be a matched pair or, at least, two cups that were presented as a pair to the Japanese court. For whatever reason, one of the pair was buried with Emperor Ankan and the other ended up in the Shōsō-in. They'll be brought together again after a separation of fourteen hundred years, and in only three days. What do you think of that?"

There was a certain beauty—a physical purity, if you will, with no trace of clammy sentiment—in two insentient objects, cut-glass pieces of foreign origin, describing two lines which fate would bring together after a separation of some fourteen hundred years. Even I, certainly no specialist, was fascinated. Of course my fascination had been inspired in large measure by Kuwashima's infectious enthusiasm.

"I'd like to see it," I said to him. "I hope you won't mind if I go with you."

I took a room at a small inn on Mt. Yoshida and spent most of the morning looking at the rough-barked pines that grew on the slopes. The view was familiar. As a student I had lived in a rooming house nearby for about a year. In the afternoon I went downtown, and then by streetcar to the western outskirts of the city, where I walked from the Kitano Shrine to the Tōji-in. Then I returned to the inn. In my student days, I often spent my Sundays thus, in the heart of the city and then in the relative calm of Kitano.

The evening was cloudy and threatening, but later in the night there was a cold, bright moon in the clear sky.

The next day I met Kuwashima at Kyoto station, and we went by train to Osaka and then on to Fusé. I intended to coordinate my activities with Kuwashima's during the two days we would be together. Kuwashima planned first to call on Mr. N of Fusé and have him show us the glass cup, which had been found among his family possessions. In the afternoon we would visit Ankan's tomb, the site of the Sairin-ji, and the house of a family named Morita, all in Furuichi. The Morita house had been the residence of the Kamiya family, known to have owned the cup during the Edo Period. This schedule of activities had not been drawn up especially for my benefit. Kuwashima evidently wished to visit these several places. At first I had been concerned lest he waste his valuable time on me.

"Don't worry," he said. "No scholar would dream of playing guide to a vacationing friend. You're the type who would. I suppose that's the reason you couldn't become one of us. But you've managed to stay out of the poorhouse."

I saw that he had on a pair of army boots and an old pair of tuxedo trousers. Indeed he looked as if he might have come straight from a poorhouse. Yet he radiated a kind of personal immaculacy.

While we were waiting in the sitting room of Mr. N, the head of an old family in Fusé, Kuwashima told me of the curious circumstances that had led to the rediscovery of the cup. During the summer, Professor I of Tokyo had been invited to Osaka to present a public lecture on "The Sairin-ji of Kawachi during the Asuka Period." The event was sponsored by the Society for the Study of Local Culture in Kawachi, of which Kuwashima was an influential member. After the lecture, Mr. N, a young man, walked in with a curio for the archaeologists to identify.

"I was amazed," Kuwashima said, "to think that a once-famous treasure of the Sairin-ji should reappear on the very day of a special lecture on the Sairin-ji. The Buddha must have had a hand in it."

Presently Mr. N came in with a parcel, which he set before us. Kuwashima handled it as though it were sacred. Inside the cloth wrapping was a box made of light paulownia wood, and inside was a smaller box wrapped in a worn fabric. Though Kuwashima had seen the cup only three months before, he seemed as excited as if he were seeing it for the first time. He opened the second box and lifted out a cloth pouch, and from it took out a glass cup that had been broken into ten fragments and pieced back together with adhesive lacquer. The glass, tinted a light amber, was itself a thing of beauty. Kuwashima handed the cup to me; I held it against the light from the garden and saw fine bubbles in the glass. This was the cup that had belonged to Emperor Ankan! But what struck me was the unexpected modernity.

The lid of the black-lacquered inner box was embellished with the words "Treasured Bowl" in gold overlay. An inscription, also in gold, stated that these words had been written in 1796 by "His Eminence, the Abbot"; the inscription was by one Kamo Yasutaka, who Kuwashima said was none other than Okamoto Yasutaka, one of the famous calligraphers in history.

He explained further that research has shown that "His Eminence" refers to an imperial prince, Abbot Einin of the Shōgo-in Monastery. When our young host left the room, Kuwashima told me that the N family had for many generations been headmen of the town. In the Meiji Period one of its members had served as county governor, and valuable objects such as this cup would rather naturally have come into its possession.

We left the N family home after an hour, returned to Osaka, and transferred to a suburban line. A thirty-minute ride brought us to Furuichi. It was already three in the afternoon. Given the shortness of the day in late autumn, we feared we might not have time to see Ankan's tomb. To save time we would merely walk past the site of the Sairin-ji. The Morita house, however, was said to be several centuries old and of historical importance. We took a quick look around the cold, earth-floored entranceway. I had not been especially affected by the Opaline Cup, a rather ordinary object though surprisingly modern in design, but here I was awed by the magnificence of the huge, crisscrossing beams high overhead and the cold venerability of the spacious room.

In Furuichi there were other houses built like the Moritas', with mud walls and low roof lines, like those I had seen in North China, giving the area a suggestion of what might have been a settlement of Koreans who had migrated to Japan ages ago. But the roads, whitish and stark amidst the surrounding drabness, were those of a rural Japanese town.

Kuwashima and I took a leisurely stroll through this picturesque town and walked on toward Ankan's tomb. The point at which the old road met the new thoroughfare was an elevation that commanded a panorama of the Kawachi plain around Furuichi.

"This whole area was once the burial grounds of the Yamato imperial court," Kuwashima said. Most of the knolls, islands dotting the expanse of the plain, were burial mounds. "Emperor Yūryaku, Emperor Ōjin, Emperor Chūai, Emperor Seinei . . ." One after another Kuwashima pointed out the ancient tombs, which to me were indistinguishable from ordinary tree-covered hillocks. Although the tombs had once had distinctive shapes, they were badly eroded, densely overgrown, and assimilated into their natural surroundings. We were at the center of the Furuichi group, the largest of all concentrations of ancient burial mounds, and the view that stretched away from us in all directions seemed cold and cheerless.

The weather had been menacing all afternoon. By the time we reached Ankan's tomb, the veil of rain that had been moving in from the north was suddenly upon us.

We disregarded the downpour as we surveyed the rise surmounted by the tomb. Doubtless the tomb had originally encompassed the entire rise, but the high ground was now largely farmhouses and fields along a wide road across the rise. The area now designated as the tomb was only a small part of the high ground.

During the wars of the late medieval period, the Hatakeyama clan had fortified this burial mound and called it the Takao Castle. This high ground, said Kuwashima, had since been called the Takao Rise. The donjon had stood over the center of the burial mound. The moat that now surrounded Ankan's tomb was originally a defensive moat inside the grounds of the fortress.

Kuwashima believed that the Opaline Cup had been unearthed accidentally or by looters not during the Genroku Period but a century earlier, when the Hatakeyama donjon was burned to the ground by the victorious Oda forces. As I strolled the high ground in the rain, I thought sadly how even Ankan's tomb, where the precious cup had lain undisturbed for more than a millennium, should have been a victim of the vicissitudes of war.

Having worshiped at the tomb and viewed it from all sides, we walked the short distance to Princess Kasuga's tomb. We were alone. The few brightly tinged trees about the tomb stood heavy with raindrops.

We spent almost an hour walking around the somewhat elevated tombs, occasionally seeking shelter beneath the trees. Kuwashima left me to have another look at an area at the rear of Ankan's tomb where he thought the cup might have been unearthed. He walked off briskly, his coat collar turned up. I took shelter under a tree a short distance from the road and stood there a long while waiting for him to return. I saw a column of rain sweep past the tombs. The dense forest coverings of the burial mounds stirred as if of their own will. I once saw the maelstroms of the straits of Shikoku. The stirring that seemed to come from deep within the mounds reminded me of that which emanates from deep within the vortex of a giant whirlpool.

Very suddenly I remembered that the remains of two noble figures of antiquity lay beneath those groves. "Down the river of Hatsusé, hidden amid mountains..." The mute music of the princess's sad song had, one day many centuries past, sounded through the leaves and boughs hereabouts.

※

Soaked through we took a room at a small inn just outside Furuichi, though we had planned to spend the night at a friend's house in Osaka. The cut-glass cups—one from Ankan's tomb, the other from the Shōsō-in—were to be exhibited side by side the next day in Nara. If we left early in the morning we could easily be in Nara for the display.

We had had a full day and we were tired. Our room was dank and dimly lit. The window had no shutters, and the rain pelted the glass panes.

When I finished the decanter of saké that had been served along with the dinner I was suddenly very tired. It seemed an effort even to lift a teacup. But the saké had had quite the opposite effect on Kuwashima, who seemed to have come to life. He sat with a row of empty decanters on his tray.

"Don't wait for me, go on to sleep," he urged repeatedly. We could have talked endlessly, and so around nine o'clock I had the maid spread bedding and lay down.

Kuwashima continued talking, glancing at me occasionally to see whether I was listening. "I'm convinced," he said, "that the two glass cups are products of the Sassanid Dynasty of Persia. They were brought over the Pamirs, across the Takla Makan Desert of the Tarim Basin and along the Silk Road to China, and eventually brought to Japan through Paekche on the Korean Peninsula. That would have been during the reign of Emperor Ankan, or when he was crown prince perhaps." Drink made him more talkative. "One of the pair was presented to Emperor Ankan, the other to his consort."

"Really?"

"That's what I think. Don't mind my talking. It's about the only pleasure we archaeologists have. When I'm drinking and think about these things I tend to forget about the war and what it has brought us. The princess was young and beautiful. It's a fact that she was young, much younger than the emperor. We have record of it. The princess's cup was stolen."

"How did that happen?"

"What I have to say is a blend of fact and speculation. *The Chronicle* mentions the theft of her jewel necklace. What was called a necklace might well have been the cup. Let's assume that the stolen cup was sold to some unsuspecting rich man, later presented by his descendant to Emperor Shōmu, and then placed in the Shōsō-in along with Shōmu's other possessions. The other cup was buried with Emperor Ankan. Centuries later a fortress was built on the burial mound. During a battle three hundred years later the fortress was burned down. There was a storm, and the next morning a farmer noticed that a section of the bare grounds had been washed away. He saw something that glittered and tried to dig it up. But in the process his pick struck the glittering object and broke it into ten fragments. Because it was obviously something of value, he collected the pieces and took them to the village headman's house, which is the house we saw today."

He seemed almost in a state of ecstasy. I listened nostalgically, for it was the Kuwashima of our student days, catching us all in the spell of his narrative.

"Are your lectures like this?" I asked.

"I suppose so. That's more or less the way it is in archaeology. Just keep listening. And then . . ."

His voice seemed to fuse with the rain and to fade into the distance. I was asleep.

I awoke in the middle of the night and saw that the dinner trays had been taken away. Kuwashima was asleep, breathing lightly, in the next bed.

The rain had stopped. It was perfectly still outside. Because I had fallen asleep so early, my mind was clear. My watch showed that it was barely two in the morning. I tried to go back to sleep.

As I lay in the dark, I recalled Kuwashima's imaginative tale of the two cups, heard in indistinct snatches as I fell asleep. The more I thought of it the more likely it seemed. He had said the cup was stolen from the princess. The cup in my mind became a symbol of the princess's love. When it vanished, so too, I thought, did her love. Perhaps because she had lost the cup she could feel only the impersonal grief, as Kizu had suggested, expressed in her elegy, "Down the river of Hatsusé, hidden amid mountains . . ."

I thought of the cups brought together after long separation. Each symbolized the love of its owner, and tomorrow they would be joined, in symbolic resurrection of that lost love. I thought on and on, enlarging upon the theme.

The next day was fine. When we left the inn at eight it was very cold, as if winter were already upon us.

"I kept on drinking by myself last night," Kuwashima said as we walked to the station. "I seem to be happiest when I'm drinking. Perhaps it's a sign that I'm at the end of the road as a scholar." He laughed quietly.

We went to Osaka and then to Nara by rail. We were two hours early and took a stroll about the city.

It was well past two when the cut-glass cup, brought from the repository shelf where it had languished for twelve centuries, and the Opaline Cup, brought that day from Fusé, were placed together on a crimson carpet just off the main hallway of the Shōsō-in. Present were only Professor U and others of the Department of Archaeology of Kyoto University, a few persons affiliated with the Shōsō-in, and myself.

I stood somewhat aside, not wanting to be in the way, and looked over the shoulders of the experts.

Because I had been looking out at the sunlit grounds while the cups were being arranged, I could not at first make them out at all. My eyes soon adjusted to the dimness, and when the crimson resumed its original brightness I saw two glass cups, surely identical, one almost touching the other.

Professor U bent over for a close look. Kuwashima, opposite him, was looking straight down, and the three young research assistants were for a time frozen in poses of eager attention.

I wanted to be witness to the instant of intersection. Two lines had moved eastward from a Persian lakeshore, erratically crossed the hemisphere, and then parted for a very long span of time.

I looked at the star-like brilliance of the incised discs. The Opaline Cup, like its mate, was a cluster of some thirty incisions, glittering a faint crimson. The two cups, for all their brilliance, were images of serenity.

I heard water brimming over. I was certain of it. I looked away for a moment, but the sound had vanished.

Perhaps it was the overflowing of a vessel beneath the floor. I had heard the sound distinctly and was surprised that no one else had.

I glanced again at the crimson carpet and saw two glass cups tinted a light amber. They were quite different from those I had seen there a moment earlier. The cups before had seemed larger and of a brilliant hue. Their crimson glitter had, of course, been due to the refraction of the crimson carpet. The angle had been right for it.

Still looking over shoulders, I studied the cups. They were not the brilliant objects I had first seen.

I no longer wanted to look at them. It was enough to have seen them in their fullest beauty, to a pure, clean sound of water. I would profit no more from them.

I signaled to Kuwashima that I was stepping outside, and left the Shōsō-in. He and the others had just begun examining the cups. Having some time to myself, I strolled down a narrow road, dark in the shadows of trees.

I thought of the tombs of Ankan and Princess Kasuga, rising over the Kawachi plain. On a day like this they would be utterly calm. I visualized them in the cold, quiet autumn landscape.

And I thought of the Kizu family graves on Shōdo Island, on a rise over the Inland Sea. I had twice visited that island off the coast of Shikoku, for the funerals of Kizu and my sister. The one small tombstone would be wet in this time of rains. Would Kizu and Tao finally be brought together, even as the cups had been? Only then would the sadness vanish. Having come this far, I said to myself, I must go on to Shōdo Island. I have not visited that rise over the Inland Sea since the end of the war.

The Rhododendrons

Translated by
Edward Seidensticker

How quickly time passes. It is five years since I was last here at Katada. Five years have gone by since that spring, the spring of 1944, when we had begun to see that the war was not going well. It seems like many years ago, and it seems like yesterday. Sometimes I think I am less sensitive to time than I once was. When I was young it was different. In the *Anatomy Magazine* last month someone called me a vigorous old gentleman of eighty. I am not, though. I still have two years to go, but I suppose I must strike people as an "old gentleman." I don't like that expression. There is something a little too warm and mellow about it. I would much rather be called an old scholar. Miike Shuntarō, old scholar.

"There are more famous spots for viewing Lake Biwa than you can count on your fingers," the owner of this inn used to say, "but there is no place along the entire lake shore that is better than Katada for viewing Mt. Hira." In particular, he liked to boast that no view of Hira could compare with the one from the northeast room of the Reihōkan Inn itself. Indeed the Reihōkan, "Inn of the Holy Mount," takes its name from the fact that Hira viewed from here looks its grandest and most god-like. The view is not like that from Hikoné, with Hira sweeping the horizon east to west, the very essence of the great mountain mass; but from here it has a dignity and character you do not find in ordinary mountains. Calmly enfolding those deep valleys, the summit more often than not hidden in clouds, it sweeps down to plant its foot solidly on the shore of the lake. There is no denying its beauty.

How long has the old innkeeper been dead, I wonder. Twenty years?—no, longer. The second time I came here, over the Keisuké affair, he was already paralyzed and had trouble speaking, and it must have been very soon afterwards, possibly two or three months, that I had notice of his death. He seemed like a worn-out old man to me then, but he could not have been over seventy. Already I have lived almost ten years longer than he did.

Nothing in the inn has changed. I was twenty-four or twenty-five when I first came here. Fifty years have somehow gone by since I first sat in this room. It is strange for a house to have gone unchanged for fifty years. The young owner is the image of his father, and he sits in the same dark office off the hall, his expressions and his mannerisms exactly like the old man's. The landscape painting in the musty alcove here and the statue under it might for all I know be the ones that were here then. Everything has changed at home. Furniture, people, the way people think. I know of nothing that has not changed. A steady change, from year to year, from month to month—from moment to moment and from second to second, it might be better to say. There cannot be many houses where change is so constant. It is intolerable. I put a chair out on the veranda and I can be sure that in an hour it will be facing another direction.

What a calm, quiet place this is! And how many years has it been since I was last able to relax so completely? The scholar's hour. I sit on the veranda with no one watching me. I look at the lake. I look at Hira. No one turns a malicious eye toward me, no brassy voices jar on my nerves. If I want a cup of hot tea I clap for the maid. Probably if I were not to clap I would see no one until time for dinner. I do not hear a radio. Or a phonograph or a piano. I do not hear that shrill voice of Haruko's or the voices of those wild grandchildren. Or Hiroyuki's voice—he has become a little insolent these last few years.

In any case, they must be quite upset by now, probably in an uproar because I disappeared without a word. I have stopped going out alone as I have grown older, never knowing when the worst might happen. And now I have been missing for more than five hours. Even Haruko will be upset. "The old man has disappeared, the old man has disappeared," she'll be saying in that shrill voice as she hunts around the neighborhood and asks whether anyone has seen me. Hiroyuki will have been called home from the office, but, being Hiroyuki, he'll not have wanted to call the police or tell the relatives. He'll have telephoned people and found not a trace of me, and he'll be pacing the floor with a sour expression on his face. But he's a worrier. Maybe he'll have called at least his brother and sister. Sadamitsu will have come from the university, and he'll be at my desk drinking tea and scowling to show how much he resents having been bothered. Kyōko will have hurried over from Kitano. Sadamitsu and Kyōko never show their faces unless something like this happens. I suppose they are busy, but it wouldn't hurt them now and then to come around and bring a little candy or fruit to the only parent they have left. For six months or a year on end they would forget all about me if I didn't remind them, that's how little the two of them know of their duty as children.

Let them worry until tomorrow. Tomorrow at noon I'll be back as if I had never been away. I still have my rights, even if I am seventy-eight. I can go out alone if I want to. I have the rights that are so fashionable these days. I don't see why it should be wrong for me to go out without telling everyone. I used to be a good drinker in my younger days, and I would spend a night here and a night there without saying a word to Misa. Sometimes I would stay away for three or four nights running, and not once did I call up the house, as Hiroyuki is always doing, to say I wouldn't be home. Haruko has him under her thumb. He's too soft with her and he's too soft with the children. I don't like it at all.

I don't suppose, though, that we'll get by without a quarrel when I do go back tomorrow. This is what I mean, this is why it wears me out so to take care of him, Haruko will say in a voice loud enough for Sadamitsu and Kyōko to hear. And since Haruko is Haruko, she might even throw herself down and weep for them, just to make herself amply disagreeable. The others will have to tell me too how they stayed awake the whole night worrying. But I won't say a word. I'll just look quietly from face to face, and I'll march into my study. Hiroyuki will follow me. He'll put on a sober expression, and tell me that they'd rather not have any more of my perverseness in the future. "How old do you think you are?" he'll say. "Think of your age. We can't have you doing this sort of thing. It doesn't look good." And he'll tell me how peevish and irritable I'm becoming. Let him talk. I won't say a word. I won't say a word, and I'll look at the photograph on the wall of Professor Schalbe, at those quiet eyes, filled with gentleness and charity. When I have calmed myself, I'll open my notebook and go to work on Part Nine of *Arterinsystem der Japaner*. My pen will run on.

"Im Jahre 1896 bin ich in der Anatomie und Anthropologie mit einer Anschauung hervorgetreten, indem ich behauptete . . ."

"In the year 1896 I came forth with new views in anatomy and anthropology. I held that . . ." They won't have any idea what I've written. None of them will understand that in this preface shines the immortal glory of Miike Shuntarō, scholar. Hiroyuki couldn't understand a word of it if he tried. I don't know how many years of German he had in school, but there are few who are as good at forgetting as Hiroyuki is. Sadamitsu is translating Goethe, and I suppose he might be able to read it. But then maybe he can't read anything except Goethe—he's been that way since he was very young. You can't be sure even about his Goethe. I know nothing of Goethe the writer, but I suppose Sadamitsu has succeeded in making his Goethe hard to live with. Goethe the poet can't have wanted as much as Sadamitsu does to have everything his way, refusing even to see his father and his brother and sister. All Sadamitsu knows about is Goethe, and he doesn't care whether his own father is alive or dead. He can have no idea, not the slightest, of the meaning, the scholarly value, of this study of the Japanese circulatory system, this modest but important work in non-osseous anthropology. When it comes to Hiroyuki—the others too, Haruko, Kyōko, Kyōko's husband Takatsu—I suppose the view is that a hundred-yen bill is more important than a line of my writing. They're proud enough for all that of the vulgar prestige that goes with my name, member of the Japan Academy, recipient of the X Prize, Dean of the Q University Medical School. They haul my name out in public so often that I'm almost ashamed for them. That is very well. Let them, if they like. But if it is such an honor to be my children, they might make an effort to understand me, they might be a little more considerate.

Possibly Yokoya and Sugiyama at the university have been told that I'm missing. They'll wonder if I've gone away to die. Will they think I've decided to kill myself out of disgust with the times, or will they think I don't want to live any longer because my research is not going as well as it might? If Keisuké were living, he at least might understand. Looking at me with those clean, gentle eyes, he would come nearer than anyone to understanding. He was my eldest son. He grew up when I was living in a tenement, and he was sensitive to things as the others have never been. Even to his father it was plain that he was unusually subtle and discerning.

If pressed, though, I would have to admit that I did not like Keisuké as well as the others. He never was near me, he never climbed on my knee, maybe because I was studying in Germany during the years when he began to take notice of the world. I can't help thinking, though, that if Keisuké were alive he would understand. He would eye me coolly, but he would arrange somehow to make me feel a little less unhappy.

But I won't kill myself. *The Arterial System of the Japanese* has yet to be finished. The work that I shall not finish if I live to be a hundred, the arduous and thankless work that no one can continue when I die, is waiting for me. My life is irreplaceable, and only I in all the world know its value. Very probably—I may be the only person in the world. In 1909 at the Anthropological Congress in Berlin, Professor Cracci said he placed a higher value on Miike the scholar than even Miike did, and he hoped that Miike would be kind to himself. The calmest and cleanest words of praise I have ever heard, and they were for me. But Professor Cracci is dead. So are Sakura and Iguchi. Sakura and Iguchi saw the value of my work, it seemed, but they were remarkable men themselves. It's been a very long time now since the academic world last heard of them, splendid though their work was. Probably I'm the only person left who can see it for what it was.

Why did I suddenly want to come to Katada? The impulse seems strange indeed. I wanted more than I can say to be in the northwest room of the Reihōkan looking at the lake. I wanted so much to look up from the lake to Hira that I could not control myself. It was the matter of the money that set me off, of course, but my real reason had nothing to do with such trivia.

Yesterday I asked Hiroyuki for the twelve thousand yen they had from selling part of the stock of paper I had stored in the basement at the university. Hiroyuki gave me a sour, twisted look. He sees to most of my expenses, and, life not being easy these days, it no doubt seemed natural that the money from my paper should go to him. But I couldn't agree. The paper was for publishing Volume Three of what is literally my life's work, *Arterin-system der Japaner*. It is paper that I would not trade for anything in the world, paper that I bought during the war with money I somehow managed to scrape together, and stored at the university when it seemed that we would be bombed. It is not like paper that would go into publishing worthless novels or dictionaries. The result of fifty years' labor by Miike Shuntarō, founder of non-osseous anthropology, printed, and, if the times were but normal, distributed to every university and every library in the world. It is not just ordinary paper. It is paper on which my life, turned to several million words of German, should be printed. I wanted to put the money away in my desk, so that I could go on with my work feeling at least the slight repose it would bring. Though I have been poor all my life, I have never let myself feel poor. I have had to borrow, but I have bought what I wanted, and eaten what I wanted, and I have drunk each day as though saké were meant to swim in. Is it really possible to be poor and at the same time a scholar? People who have never been scholars cannot judge.

I let word slip out about the paper, and Hiroyuki and Haruko set their eyes on it. If I had said nothing, they could hardly have had ideas about making money from my paper.

It's my money. I won't have them laying their hands on a single yen of it. So I said to Hiroyuki. I was not being unpleasant and I was not being selfish. I was only saying what I meant.

"You might be a little more cooperative, Father," Hiroyuki said, and with that I lost my temper.

If he had come and asked me humbly for the money, I might have reconsidered on the spot. "We're having a hard time of it, Father," he might have said. "Forgive us for asking, but could you let us have part of the money?" I might not have given up as much as half of it, but I would have let him have possibly a fifth.

Haruko poked her head in from the dining room: "Father is right. It's his money. It would be best to give it to him, every last cent of it." She was polite in a very icy way.

"That's right. It's my money. I won't have it being wasted on candy for those children."

Hiroyuki snorted. Let him snort—I don't care if he is my son, that sort of double-dealing is intolerable. If Misa were alive, I would not be driven to this. Misa tended to be weak, though, and toward the end she was taking their part. I could not depend on her. But when it came to money from paper that was to go into my work she would not have given in easily. I feel sure of that.

What happened this morning only made matters worse. I was at my desk, ready to begin work, when Haruko came in with a roll of bills, twelve thousand yen. That was very well, but she didn't have to say what she did: "You're getting to be very fond of money, aren't you, Father?"

I am not fond of money. I am seventy-eight years old, and I have lived a life of honest poverty with my studies. I have had nothing besides scholarship. If I had wanted money, I would have become a clinician, and presently I would have opened my own practice, and by now I would be a rich man. I would not have spent my time prodding corpses in a dark laboratory, begging rich businessmen for donations, writing books in foreign languages and not selling a copy. Haruko was as wrong as she could be. There's a limit to this obtuseness. Having to live in such a vulgar atmosphere, in the house of an ordinary office worker with not the slightest scholarly ties, and, the times being what they are, having to depend on his insignificant salary, how can I rest easy without money of my own, however little it may be, tucked away in my desk? I can't relax with my work. And they seem to resent the fact that I don't turn over my pension to help pay household expenses. But if I were to do that, where would I find the money to pay the students who help me? That pension is all the money I have for my research. Isn't it really going too far when a son sets his eye on his own father's pension?

THE RHODODENDRONS

I did not answer Haruko. I did not want to dirty my mouth with a single word. I took the twelve thousand yen from her, and counted it with quivering hands, bill by bill, right under her eyes. It was exactly right: a hundred twenty bills.

"Very well. You may go now," I said.

I sat for a time at my desk. I made myself a bowl of tea. I held the old Hagi tea bowl (it was left on my seventieth birthday by a student who did not give his name—I like both the bowl and the student, whoever he was) at my chest, and tilted it so that the rich green foam trailed off down the side.

I looked out at the garden. Beyond the shrubbery I saw a slovenly figure in Western clothes coming in from the gate. It was the manager of the Ōmoriya Dry Goods Store. I had seen him two or three times before. Probably Haruko was selling another kimono. She brought her clothes with her when she was married, and she can sell them if she likes. We are not that hard up yet, however. If we were, we could stop those piano lessons for Yūichi. What possible good does it do to spend a lot of money giving piano lessons to a twelve-year-old boy who has no real talent? And how annoying that piano is! Music is for a genius to give his life to. The painting lessons for Keiko, who is only eight, are the same. Complete, absolute waste! They talk about "educating the sensibilities." Educating the sensibilities! Education of the sensibilities is a far different thing. How can they educate the sensibilities without teaching a decent respect for scholarship?

The useless expenses on the children are one example, but there are plenty of others. Haruko was saying the other day that she had her shoes shined at Shijō, and it cost her twenty yen. Shocking! But did Hiroyuki reprimand her for it? By no means. He said that he himself had his shoes shined in front of Kyōgoku. It cost him thirty yen, but the shoe-shine boys at Kyōgoku were politer and more thorough. An able-bodied man and woman hiring someone to shine their shoes! What can one possibly say?

THE RHODODENDRONS

And then they complain that they have trouble making ends meet, and they sell their clothes. Their whole way of thinking is riddled with inconsistencies. If the husband drank, if he drank like a fish, and that made it hard to pay the bills, I would understand. My life as a matter of fact has been a succession of days when drinking made it hard to pay the bills. Research and liquor. The dissecting room and the bar. But the money I spent on liquor was different, even if you must call it waste. I would never economize on liquor to have my shoes shined. I would probably go on drinking even if I had to shine someone else's shoes. Liquor is one of my basic needs. Like my research, it makes its demands and there is no putting it off.

As I heard the man from the Ōmoriya ringing the door bell, I got up and changed clothes. Across my chest I strung the decoration I am most fond of, the little Order of the Red Cross, First Degree, given to me by the Polish Government. With the beginning of Part Nine and a German dictionary in my brief case, I stepped down from the veranda into the garden. I first put the twelve thousand yen in an outside pocket, then moved it to my breast pocket. I cut across the garden and went out through the back gate. Perhaps because I was angry, my knee joint creaked at each step.

I walked slowly out to the streetcar track, where I was lucky enough to stop a taxi. I asked how much the fare would be to Katada. It would be possibly two hundred yen, I thought, but the driver, who could not have been more than eighteen or nineteen, said two thousand. I was furious. My hands shook. The driver spun the wheel as though he thought me a complete fool, but I called after him. "All right, take me to Katada." He turned around and opened the door from inside. In the old days a driver would have climbed out to open the door.

The taxi shook violently. "This will never do," I said to myself. I told the driver to slow down. I closed my eyes, folded my arms, and hunched my shoulders, contracting the exposed surface of my heart to lessen the burden on it. The shaking subsided as we moved out of Kyoto and onto the concrete surface of the Ōtsu highway. Over the pass at Keagé and down into Yamashina and Ōtsu. From Ōtsu the road turned north along the lake shore, and Hira lay before us. Ah, Hira! my heart sang. I had almost unconsciously told the driver that I wanted to go to Katada, and the impulse had not been wrong. I did indeed want to see Lake Biwa, and Hira. I wanted to stand on the veranda of the Reihōkan, all by myself, and look at the quiet waters of Lake Biwa and at Mt. Hira beyond until I was content.

⚜

I was twenty-five when I first saw Hira. Some years before, I had come upon a copy of *Picture News*, a magazine but recently founded. I was still a high school student in Tokyo, and the magazine belonged to my landlady's daughter. The frontispiece, in the violet tint popular then, was captioned "The Rhododendrons of Hira."

I remember the picture vividly even now. It was taken from the summit of Hira, with a corner of Lake Biwa like a mirror far below. Down over the steep slope, broken here and there by a boulder, stretched a brilliant field of mountain rhododendrons. A sort of astonishment swept over me, I have no idea why. A volatile, ether-like excitement stirred a corner of my heart. Carefully I studied the picture of the rhododendrons of Hira.

I said to myself that someday I would stand on the little steamer, depicted in a circular inset on the same page, that several times each day made its way from hamlet to hamlet up the lake coast; and, looking up at the jagged lines of Hira, I would climb to exactly the spot on the peak from which the picture was taken. I do not know how to explain it, but I was quite sure that the day would come. It would come. Without fail. My heart had made its decision, shall we say—in any case, I felt not the slightest doubt.

THE RHODODENDRONS

And I thought too that the day when I would climb Hira would be a lonely day for me. How shall I describe it? A day when I had to be moving, when no one understood me. "Solitary" is a convenient word. Or perhaps "despairing" will do. Solitary, despairing. In general I dislike such dandyisms, but I can't help thinking that here they fit the case. On a day of solitude and despair, I would climb to the summit of Hira, where the mountain rhododendrons would be in bloom, and I would lie down by myself and sleep under the heavily scented clusters of flowers. That day would come. It had to come. My confidence, as I look back on it, seems so passive that I find it hard to understand, but at the time it moved into my heart as the most proper and acceptable thing in the world. So it was that I first came to know of Hira.

Some years later I saw not a picture but the real Hira. I was twenty-five, I think. It was the end of the year after I graduated from the Imperial University, and I was lecturing at the Okayama Medical College. That would make it 1896. An angel of death was with me in those days. Everyone goes through some such period when he is young, and life hardly seems worth living. Keisuké was twenty-five when he died so senselessly. If he had lived through the crisis, he would probably have had tens of years ahead of him. Spineless, irresolute Keisuké—but the angel of death that was after him may have been a stronger one than mine. What a fool he was, though—and yet one couldn't help feeling sorry for him. If he were alive today—the fool, the fool. The unspeakable fool. When I think of Keisuké, my temper quite gets the better of me.

The angel of death that followed me when I was twenty-five was a simpler one than Keisuké's. I had doubts about the meaning of my existence, and I thought of ending it, that was all. I had not yet come upon my life's work, non-osseous anthropology. I can see now that my heart was full of chinks. I was saturated in religion and philosophy as no student of the natural sciences should be. It was some years later that Fujimura Masao threw himself over Kegon Falls, but every student who went into philosophy and such was at some time or other threatened by much the same angel of death. "The truth is exhausted in one word, 'incomprehensible' "—it was a strange age, and we seriously thought such thoughts. A strange age, when the youth of the nation was lost in meditation on problems of life and death.

Winter vacation came. I went straight to Kyoto with a Zen text under my arm, and into the Tenryū-ji temple at Saga. There, with an old sage for my master, I threw myself into Zen meditation. Almost every night I sat on the veranda of the main hall. Sometimes I went out to sit on a boulder by the lake, which was covered each night with a thin sheet of ice. When we finished the all-night services celebrating the Buddha's enlightenment, I was staggering with exhaustion. I can see now that there was nothing in the world the matter with me but a bad case of nerves from malnutrition and over-work and lack of sleep.

It was the morning of the twenty-second or twenty-third of December, whichever day the winter solstice was that year. As soon as the services were over, I left the Tenryū-ji and started for Ōtsu. I suppose it was about eight o'clock in the morning. The tree stumps in the temple precincts were covered lightly with snow, and it was a cold morning even for Saga, a morning to freeze the nose and ears. In my cotton priest's robe, my bare feet slipped into sandals, I walked as fast as I could through Kitano and the main part of Kyoto, and on to Ōtsu, not once stopping to rest, over the road I took today. I remember that a light snow was falling when I passed the Kaneyo restaurant in Yamashina. I was nearly fainting with hunger.

Why do you suppose I went to Ōtsu? The details are no longer very clear in my mind. It would be a distortion to say that I was attracted to Hira by the picture I had seen in *Picture*

News years before. Probably I started out with a vague intention of finding a place on the shore of the lake to die. Or possibly I simply moved toward the lake like a sleepwalker, and as I looked out over the water the thought of dying came to me.

It was a very cold day. At Ōtsu I turned and walked up the lake, the angel of death with me. On my right the cold water stretched motionless, on and on. Now and then a few birds started up from among the reeds near the shore.

In front of me was Mt. Hiei, and to the left and far beyond soared a line of peaks white with snow, their beauty a revelation. I was used to the gentler lines of the mountains around Saga with their scattered groves of trees, and the harsh, grand beauty of these mountains was a change to make me wonder that the word "mountain" could cover both. I must have asked a peddler along the way—in any case I knew that the range before me was Hira. Now and then I stopped to look at Hira, and the angel of death looked with me. I was held captive by those jagged lines stretching off into the distance, almost god-like.

It was evening when I reached the Floating Hall in Katada. From time to time through the day a few flakes of snow had fallen. Now it began snowing in earnest, and the air was dense with snowflakes. I stood for a long time under the eaves of the Floating Hall. The surface of the lake was cut off from view. I took out my purse and undid the strings with freezing fingers, and one five-yen bill fell out. With that clutched in my hand I stepped into the wide hall of an inn by the lake. It was a fairly imposing place, but somehow it suggested a country post-inn—the Reihōkan.

A middle-aged man with close-cropped hair was warming himself in the office. I shoved the five-yen bill at him and asked him to let me stay the night. He said I should pay in the morning, and when I made him take it he looked at me curiously. He was suddenly very kind. A maid fifteen or sixteen years old brought hot water, and as I sat down on the sill, rolled up the skirt of my robe, and soaked my toes, red and numb from the cold, I felt a little like a human being again. I was given this room, the best one in the Reihōkan. It was already so dark that I had to have a light.

I said not a word. I ate what the innkeeper's wife gave me, and, taking up my position before the alcove, I began my Zen meditations again. I had decided that the next day I would jump over the cliff beside the Floating Hall. I wondered with some disquiet whether my five-foot self would sink quietly, as a rock sinks. My drowned form at the bottom of the lake came before my eyes time after time, and I felt that I was seeing a particularly heroic death.

It was as quiet as the hall of the Tenryū-ji. The night was bitterly cold, and the slightest movement brought new stabs of cold. I sat in meditation for I do not know how many hours. Toward dawn I came to myself. I was thoroughly exhausted. I got up and went to the toilet, and then lay down to rest. Bedding had been laid out in a corner of the room, but I did not touch it. Instead I lay on the floor with my arm for a pillow. I thought I would doze off for an hour or two until daylight.

At that moment a piercing, throat-splitting scream filled the air. The cry of a night bird possibly? I raised my head and looked around, but the night was quiet as before. I was composing myself for sleep when the same scream came a second time, from under the veranda, it seemed, almost below my head. I got up, lit a lantern, went out to the veranda, and slid open the outside door. The light reached only the eaves. I could see nothing beyond. Fine snowflakes fell steadily into the narrow circle. As I leaned over the railing and tried to see into the darkness under the veranda, the scream came again, louder than before; and from directly below me, where the cliff fell away to the lake, a bird flew up with a terrible beating of wings, almost near enough to brush my cheek. I could not see it, but those wings, flying off into the snowy darkness over the lake, sounded with a violence that struck me to the heart. I stood for a time almost reeling.

The terrible energy, shall we call it the vital force, in one night bird took me so by surprise that my angel of death left me.

The next day, in heavy snow, I walked back alive to Kyoto.

⚑

I did not see Hira from Katada again until the time of the Keisuké affair. The date I cannot forget: the fall of 1926.

It was the year I became dean of the medical school, and I was fifty-five. The years from then until I retired at sixty were years of rankling unpleasantness. The Keisuké affair, Misa's death a year later, Hiroyuki's marriage and Kyōko's, both of which displeased me intensely. Then there was Sadamitsu's drift toward radicalism, and as dean of the medical school I was little more than an errand boy, forced to give up what was most important to me, my research. Each day added a new irritation.

The Keisuké affair came quite without warning. A call from R University, and Misa went to see what the difficulty was. Keisuké had been expelled because of trouble with some woman. I could not believe my ears when Misa came into my study and told me. Keisuké had always had a weak strain in him, and we had had to put him in R University, a private school without much standing, because his grades were below average; but there was something boyish about him—he had a quietness and docility lacking in the other children. I had always thought him a model of good behavior. But I suppose he showed a different face to other people, and he had proceeded to get some tramp of an eighteen-year-old waitress pregnant.

I thought the affair might just possibly have found its way into the papers, and when I opened my evening paper, there indeed it was, headlined "Student Indecencies" or something equally trite. The story of Keisuké's misbehavior, quite new to me, was told in some detail. "The son of an important educator, a dean in a certain university," the article said, giving a fictitious name that would suggest mine immediately. My standing as an educator was gone. That was very well. I had never considered myself an educator anyway. I am only a scholar. But the boy's conduct, so unbecoming in a student, was most distressing to me as a father, the only father he had, after all. I had more trouble later when Sadamitsu turned radical, but that incident at least had its redeeming features. There was not one detail I could console myself with in the Keisuké affair.

I did not leave my study until Keisuké came home later that night. I heard him in the dining room, talking to Misa in that wheedling way of his. He seemed to be eating. I could hear a clatter of dishes.

I walked down the hall and slid open the door to the dining room. Keisuké's student uniform was unbuttoned and the white lining was in full view. The sight of him there quite at his ease, with Misa to serve him, was too much for me.

"Get out of here. I won't have the likes of you around the house."

Keisuké pulled himself up. His soft eyes were turned to the floor.

I shouted at him again. "Get out of here! Get out!"

He quietly left the room and went upstairs.

I did not think he would really leave the house, but at about nine o'clock, when Misa went upstairs to look for him, he was gone.

From the next day Misa refused to eat. I thought little about the matter, however. Keisuké being Keisuké, I was sure that he would be crawling home very soon.

I have no idea how she was able to learn so much, but Misa reported that the girl, in spite of her youth, was a formidable creature indeed. She had already had one child, and she had

had no trouble in making a plaything of Keisuké.

"Whether he was the deceiver or the deceived," I answered, "the end result was the same."

Just as I had expected, a telephone call came from Keisuké. It was the third day after he had left home. Quite by accident I was looking for medical magazines in the next room, where my books were stored. I thought there was something very strange about Hiroyuki's smothered voice. I went out to the veranda, where he and Misa were whispering to each other, and asked if the call hadn't been from Keisuké. Neither of them answered for a time, but Hiroyuki finally admitted that it had been. They had apparently meant to tell me nothing. Keisuké, it seemed, was staying with the woman at the Lakeside Hotel in Sakamoto, and Hiroyuki was to take him money.

The next afternoon, brushing aside Misa's misgivings, I went by taxi to the Lakeside Hotel. I asked at the desk to have Keisuké called, and a minute or two later there was a slapping of sandals on the wide staircase before me, and a young girl appeared. Her hair was cut in bangs after the schoolgirl fashion. She wore a cheap kimono tied with a narrow reddish obi. Careless, childish if you will—in any case it was an odd way to be dressed. She came halfway downstairs and threw a glance in my direction, and when she saw who it was her expression quickly changed. She stared at me for a moment with wide, round eyes, then turned and ran back upstairs with a lightness that made me think of a squirrel. It was hard to believe that she was pregnant.

Another minute passed and a worried-looking Keisuké came down. I went with him into the lobby, where we sat facing each other over a table. I handed him the money he had asked for.

"You are to go home today. You are not to go out of the house for the time being. You are not to see that woman again. Misa will take care of her."

"But . . ." Keisuké hesitated.

"You are to go home today," I said again.

Keisuké asked me to let him think the matter over until the next day. I was so furious that I shook, but I could say nothing. There seemed to be a wedding reception somewhere in the hotel, and people in formal clothes were giving us vaguely curious glances. I stood up.

"Very well. You have your choice. Either that worthless woman or your own father."

I ordered him to come to Katada with his answer by noon the next day.

"Yes, sir," Keisuké said quietly. "I'm sorry to have bothered you." He turned and went back upstairs. I had the man at the desk call the Reihōkan—Katada was not far away—and presently I stepped from the taxi and was back at this inn for the first time in thirty years. The Keisuké affair had exhausted me mentally and physically. The next day was Sunday, and I looked forward to a good rest.

The innkeeper came up to my room. He had aged, but I could still see in his face the face of thirty years before. I telephoned the house in Kyoto to tell Misa briefly what had happened. How many years since I had last spent a quiet evening alone, reading nothing and writing nothing? It was a little early for duck, but the fish from the lake was very good. I slept beautifully.

There was a telephone call from Kyoto at ten the next morning as I was sitting down to breakfast. The voice over the wire was not Misa's usual voice.

"Word has come from the hotel that Keisuké and the woman drowned themselves in the lake this morning. Please go to Sakamoto at once. We are just leaving the house."

I was stunned. What had the fool done? He had taken the woman and discarded me. That was very well. But did he have to pick such an unpleasant way to answer his own father?

I did not go to Sakamoto.

At about three Hiroyuki came to the inn. I was sitting on the veranda in a rattan chair, and I looked up to see Hiroyuki glaring at me, his face pale and grim.

"Don't you feel the least bit sorry for him?"

"Of course I do. I would feel sorry for anyone who could be such a fool."

"They haven't found the bodies yet. All sorts of people have been helping, and you ought to show your face." He threw the words out, and turned to leave. He had come all the way to my inn just to say that.

About an hour later Misa came, with Kyōko and Takatsu, who was then Kyōko's fiancé. Misa came into the room and started toward me as though she wanted to throw herself at my feet. Then she reconsidered and sat down in a corner, silent and motionless, her face buried in her hands. I knew that she was trying very hard to keep from sobbing.

"Maybe they will come up before evening," Takatsu said. He meant the bodies.

I disliked having him around at such a time. I had of course been opposed from the start to his marrying Kyōko. His father, the most successful or possibly the second most successful businessman in Osaka, was an uncultured upstart who cared less than nothing for scholarship. His sneering arrogance thoroughly displeased me. "I think I can see to the money for your publishing," he said the first time I met him. Misa and the children visited his house once, and I gather that the power of money swept them off their feet. "The house is enormous, and the living room is magnificent, and he has a country house at Yasé and another at Takarazuka," and so on and so on—I found the liveliness most distasteful.

That was not all. The son, Takatsu himself, had been in France for three years, but all he could talk about was the Louvre. He didn't study when he was in France and he didn't drink. All he did was wander around looking at pictures, though he was no painter. He frittered away his time. And up he came to Kyoto every Sunday, rain or snow, without waiting to see whether we would let him marry Kyōko. He's a sort I will never understand. When I said I was opposed to the marriage, Kyōko burst into tears. I was incensed. I asked how the others felt, and I found that all of them, Misa and the children, took Kyōko's part. Takatsu had apparently made a good impression on everyone but me. Neither Keisuké nor Hiroyuki had any interest in scholarship, and Sadamitsu was not to be depended upon, and I thought that at the very least I would have Kyōko marry some fine young man prepared to devote his life to scholarship. But now I was forced to give up that hope too.

In any case, I was most unhappy to see Takatsu pushing his way into an important Miike family conference, even before the wedding date had been set.

"Kyōko can go back to Sakamoto. I want to talk to her mother alone," I said.

Kyōko and Takatsu had the people at the inn make them a lunch, and called a taxi, and in general raised a commotion suggesting that the whole affair was a picnic for them.

When they had left and the room was quiet, I thought I would like to say something comforting to Misa, but instead I found myself scolding her.

"It's your fault that Keisuké has come to this. You spoiled him."

Misa sat with her head bowed, her face in her hands, so still that she might have been dead.

"Hiroyuki and Kyōko too. All of them are worthless. I have stood all I can."

Misa got up and staggered to the veranda. She put one hand to her forehead and, leaning against a pillar, looked at me. Only the one time in her life did Misa look into my eyes in that quiet way. After a time she sank to the floor as though her legs would no longer support her.

"I think at least half the fault is yours. What have you ever done for the children?"

THE RHODODENDRONS

She usually had so little to say that her talkativeness made me wonder whether the affair might not have deranged her.

"You were away in Germany when Keisuké was small. You went for three years and you stayed eight. The last five years you sent no word either to us or to the ministry. I don't think you can imagine how terrible those years were for us."

It was as Misa said. I saved the money the Ministry of Education had given me for three years' study and stayed eight years. I had no wife and no children and no house. I lived in a cheap room and ate black bread, and I kept my eye trained on scholarship, that distant eminence, lofty as the Alps. Otherwise I would not have been able to do the work I am doing today.

Misa went on. "Research, research, you say, and you have no Sundays and no holidays. When you have spare time you prod your corpses. And when you come home you say you're tired of the smell of corpses and you start drinking. You never even smile when you're drinking, and you go on writing away at that German. What have you done for the children? Have you even once looked at a report card? Have you once taken them to the zoo? You've sacrificed the children and me to that research of yours."

That I should have to hear this from Misa, who had helped me with my research through the long years of poverty, never once stopping to pamper herself!

I wanted no more of her complaining. "That's enough. I sacrificed myself too," I said.

I was staring absently at the lake, as I had been all the hours since breakfast. When I raised my eyes from the lake, there was Hira, wrapped in the deep colors of autumn, spreading its quiet form grandly before me, as if to embrace me.

"I'm going back to the hotel," said Misa coldly. She stood up and turned to leave. "I don't know what happened yesterday, but I imagine the boy died cursing you."

Perhaps she had wept herself out. Her eyes were dry, and her face was strangely composed as she arranged her shawl. She almost snatched up her bundles, and she turned her back abruptly and marched from the room as if she meant never to come back to me.

An inexpressible feeling of loneliness came over me. That will do, I said to myself, and stood up. I sat down again. I did not know what it was that would do.

⚜

I called the desk and asked for a notebook. I had not thought of him in years, but I sat down to draft a letter to Tanio Kaigetsu. Tanio Kaigetsu was neither an anatomist nor an anthropologist. For seven years I studied under Professor Schalbe at Strassburg, doing research principally on birthmarks, but also laying the foundation for my life's work, nonosseous anthropology. Afterwards I spent a year at the Leyden Museum—actually it was something of a detour for me—measuring the crania of some thousand Filipinos. A bar run by a Japanese woman was the congregating place for Japanese scholars in Leyden, and it was there that I met Tanio Kaigetsu.

He was a priest, a rather unusual priest, who was studying Sanskrit, also at the Leyden Museum. He was a little older than I, and he was a good toper—that expression fitted Tanio Kaigetsu perfectly. I was much taken with his dashing, lighthearted way of drinking. Even when he was drinking, his mind was on scholarship. I knew nothing about his research, and doubtless he knew nothing about mine, but we were exactly suited for each other. We both knew the dignity of scholarship, and we respected each other as scholars. When I left Leyden, Tanio Kaigetsu said he wanted to give me the most valuable farewell present he could. He would like to know what I needed. "Let me have your body to dissect when you die," I said.

Kaigetsu took out pen and paper on the spot, and wrote down his testament. "I give my body to the anatomist Miike Shuntarō." To his own copy he added an injunction: "My relatives are not to challenge the validity of this testament."

I had not seen Kaigetsu since I said goodbye to him in the doorway of the Leyden Museum in 1912. I knew, however, that he had come back to Japan some years after me and that he was alive and well, the resident priest in a little temple somewhere in the mountains. I was sure if I asked at the university someone would know the address of Tanio Kaigetsu, obscure old scholar of Buddhism.

I thought to get through the day by writing to Kaigetsu. The promise he had given me, I almost felt, was the only promise I had left in the world. It was the only bit of human intercourse, the only incident in my relations with mankind, in which I could have confidence.

But I sat there with pen in hand, not knowing how to begin. It seemed immeasurably difficult to communicate the warm, flowing human affection I felt for Kaigetsu after years of neglect.

I laid down my pen and looked out. The surface of the lake was aglow in the autumn twilight. Far to the east some dozens of boats were floating motionless, like fallen leaves. Keisuké and that girl—I could only think of the woman who had died with Keisuké, the woman I had seen halfway down the stairs at the Lakeside Hotel, as a young girl—the boats clustered there, I said to myself, are perhaps looking for the bodies of Keisuké and that girl.

I did not write to Kaigetsu. Instead I sat on the veranda, with the lake for my partner, trying to endure, to resist. When night came, I went back into the room and sat rigid before the desk. Now and then I stood up and looked east over the lake. There in the same spot, on into the night, were those dozens of little boats, like lights strung out for decoration.

❦

The third and most recent time I saw Hira from the Reihōkan was in the darkest days Japan has known. My heart, the heart of the nation, was plunged into a darkness that held not a fragment of hope.

We did not know when the air raids would begin, and every day the newspapers and radios were shouting at people to leave the cities. With the war situation growing worse, blackness hung ready to envelop the country. It was then, in the spring of 1944, that I was brought to Katada by Atsuko, Haruko's youngest sister. Atsuko was in her fifth year of high school. Nearly twenty years had gone by since the Keisuké affair.

I was alone in the Kyoto house with only a maid. At the beginning of the year Hiroyuki had been transferred to the Kanazawa branch of his company, and Haruko and the four children had gone with him. I say that he was transferred. Actually Hiroyuki himself had wanted very much to flee the city and the bombings, and the initiative had been his. For a man with four children, the oldest of them only eleven, I suppose this was most natural.

It apparently bothered both Hiroyuki and Haruko to leave an old man alone in Kyoto. Although they persisted in trying to make me go with them, I would have none of it. I suppose they took my refusal for the stubbornness of the old, but it was not. My work was important to me. No one, however long he argued, could pry me loose from my desk.

Hiroyuki said that my research depended on my life, but for me it was the opposite: my life depended on my research. My work was everything, and I could not proceed with my work away from the university. I had to go to the anatomy laboratory, and I could not be cut off from the libraries. If I were to leave Kyoto, my work would stop.

I could go on with my research only as long as I lived, Hiroyuki said. To me, at seventy-three, the matter was more urgent. Every morning as I sat down and began to write, a picture of my own circulatory system would float before my eyes. I knew that my veins had so degenerated that they would crumble between the fingers like scraps of biscuit. Even had there been no war, I would have been in a race against death.

THE RHODODENDRONS

Each day lived was so much gained. If things progressed smoothly, I would be ninety-three when I finished *The Arterial System of the Japanese*. I knew therefore that I could never expect to see the end of my work, and I wanted to get out the last chapter and the last sentence I could. I worked out a plan for publishing in successive volumes, each part to be sent around to the printer's as it was finished. The times were such, however, that I could not be sure when the printer would close shop.

And even if by good luck I should succeed in having several volumes published, the possibility of sending them abroad was as good as gone. I had thought, through the good offices of the German consulate in Kobe, at least to send my work to universities in the Axis countries, but it seemed that the war in Europe had succeeded in denying my last wish.

I sat at my desk those days literally begrudging the passage of each minute. I must write, and if I wrote, everything would somehow be all right. Years, tens of years after my death, by whatever devious course, my work would come to be recognized in the academic world for what it was. It would become a rock that would not wear away. Scholars would follow in my footsteps and non-osseous anthropology would be brought to maturity. So I thought, so I believed, as I drove myself on.

For all that, I often dreamed I saw my manuscript licked by flames, blazing up and dancing into the heavens with the smoke. Each time I had the dream I awoke to find my eyes wet with tears.

There was a small second-hand bookshop near the university that I used to dread going by. I knew that buried under layers of dust in one corner of the shop was a manuscript on the topography of Kyoto. I do not know who the author was, but the manuscript was written neatly in the old style on Japanese paper. It may or may not have been of value. In any case there it was, laboriously put together by someone, and, for nearly three years after I first noticed it, lying in the same corner of that bookshop, held together by a thin cord. I could not bear to think that the manuscript of *The Arterial System of the Japanese*, with its hundreds of illustrations, might have in store for it the fate of that unhappy work on Kyoto topography. I would think, as I passed, of the dark destiny that might be lying in wait for my work, and a feeling of utter desolation would come over me.

Every Sunday Atsuko came up from Ashiya. To comfort an old man working alone, she always brought wrapped in a kerchief some bread she said she had baked herself, and laid it carefully on my desk with two or three apples. Apples were not easy to find in those days.

I became rather fond of the seventeen-year-old Atsuko. There was something modest and withdrawn about her, quite the opposite of Haruko's gaudiness, and yet she was bright and open. I am not capable of affection for my grand-children, but I felt a strange warmth, a father's affection almost, for a girl who was not even one of the family. Atsuko for her part seemed to like the old man well enough.

I was walking in the garden that morning. Generally I went to work immediately after breakfast, but that morning was different. I paced the garden fretfully. The spring sun found its way through the trees to warm the earth, but I felt only a rough, harsh chill that could not be called simple anger or loneliness. I could think of nothing to do for myself but walk around the garden.

The Imperial Culture Awards had been announced with much fanfare that morning. Six men from the humanities and the natural sciences had been awarded the Culture Medal, the highest honor the nation can give its scholars.

I stared for a time at the photographs of the recipients, each with a medal on his chest, and I thought how I too would like to have a medal. I thought how I would like to be thus commended, to have my achievements written of, to have centered on me the respect and interest and understanding of the country and the people. I had never in my life envied anyone for worldly honors, but just this once, I thought, I would like to feel the weight of popular acclaim on my thin shoulders.

Was not my work greater than the work of these six men? I laid the newspaper down, went to my study, and sat at my desk. I stood up again and went out to the garden. Was my work not worth a national commendation, in all probability the last it could expect? Was my work not fit to be praised by the government, admired and respected by the people, protected? I wanted honor, now, today, I thought, however slight the honor might be. However subdued the acclaim, I wanted something to turn to.

The name Miike Shuntarō must be inscribed on men's hearts. Every last individual must be made to see the value of Miike Shuntarō's work. But there I was, at the end of my life, with the country on the verge of collapse. My thousands of pages of manuscript must be given up to no one could foresee what fate. Perhaps they would go up in smoke before my work could be recognized for what it was. Professor Schalbe—the name of the man to whom I owed so much came to my lips, and tears came to my eyes.

There was a telephone call from the administrative office at the university. The university was to give a reception the next day for Dr. K, one of the six honored scholars, and it would be appreciated if I could say a few words of congratulation on behalf of the professors emeritus. I refused.

Not five minutes later there was a call from Professor Yokoya, one of my students, with the same request.

"I have no time to write messages of congratulation about other people," I said. "I have more than enough work of my own to fill my time. I am at an age when no one need be surprised if I die tomorrow."

Yokoya was very polite and did not press the point.

I had no sooner hung up than there was a call from a newspaper reporter. He wanted a few remarks on one of the medal holders.

"I am interested in nothing except my own work. It was good of you to call, but it will not be worth your trouble to see me." With that I hung up. Since I would of course be having more calls, I left the receiver off the hook.

I went down into the garden again. For very little reason, I was overcome with a mixture of anger and sorrow and loneliness. As I paced the garden, Atsuko came in through the shrubbery. She was dressed in the drab, baggy trousers that were standard, and her face, with its young smile, was like a flower (she was indeed a flower to me then). She took out a few groceries she said had been sent by her family.

"Would you like to go to Lake Biwa?" she asked.

"Lake Biwa?" I was a little startled.

"Let's go to Lake Biwa and have a boat ride."

Even in wartime, the warmth of spring seemed to stir the young to more than everyday brightness. I found myself strangely unresisting.

"Very well. Will you take me to Lake Biwa?"

I can do nothing else today, but I can at least do what this girl wants me to. I can at least follow her—such, if I am to put them honestly, were my feelings.

We let train after train pass until finally one came with a few empty seats. We rode to Ōtsu. It was nearly twenty years since the Keisuké affair. While I was in the university and even after I retired I had chances enough to go to Ōtsu for banquets and such, but with the Keisuké affair I had come to dislike Lake Biwa and I avoided the place.

But now, brought to the lake again by Atsuko, I saw only its beauty. Time is a fearful thing. The pain of the Keisuké affair had quite faded away. The surface of the lake shimmered like fish-scales spread out in the noonday sun. Atsuko had said she wanted a boat ride, and indeed there were little rowboats and sailboats scattered over the lake. Here at least the shadow of war did not seem to fall.

As I looked out and saw Hira rising from the water, I suddenly wanted to go to Katada. A steamer was leaving just then, and the two of us climbed aboard.

A half hour later we were in Katada. We rested for a time at the Reihōkan. I saw no one I knew from the innkeeper's family, the place apparently being occupied by a single sullen maid. The windows along the hall were broken, and the inn was plainly run-down, as indeed inns were everywhere.

Atsuko helped me into a boat not far from the pier where the steamer had come in. It was my first ride in a rowboat. She borrowed a thin cushion from the boathouse for me, and showed me how to hold the sides of the boat.

There was not another boat in sight as we floated out over the water. Atsuko arched her back and strained at the oars. Perspiration broke out on her face.

"Are you enjoying yourself?" she asked.

I was in fact less than delighted, with the spray from the oars hitting me in the face and my life entrusted to a flimsy little boat.

"Thoroughly," I said. I forbade her to go into deep water, however. Cherries were blooming along the shore. The April sun carried just a touch of chill, and the clear air, free from the dust of the city, had not yet taken on the sourness of summer. Hira was beautiful.

A fish jumped up near the boat. "A fish," said Atsuko, turning to gaze with wide eyes. She slapped industriously with the oars and pulled the boat to the spot where the fish had been. I suddenly thought of the girl I had seen for but an instant halfway down the stairs at the Lakeside Hotel, the girl who had died with Keisuké. There was a trace of her in Atsuko. The exaggerated, childish surprise at the fish, the quick agility with which Atsuko brought the boat around—whatever it was, a giddiness came over me as the images of

Atsuko and the girl merged. Perhaps the girl too was fresh and clean like Atsuko. Strangely, I no longer felt angry at the girl who had taken Keisuké. Rather I was conscious of something very like affection for her, an affection which I could not feel for Keisuké himself.

I stared down into the water that buried everything, the water into which Keisuké and the girl had sunk. I pushed my hand down the side of the boat. The water slid through five thin old fingers, colder than I would have expected it to be.

Atsuko is gone. Much too soon, she died in the typhus epidemic at the end of the war. Misa is gone. Kyōko's father-in-law, whom I so disliked, is dead too. Tanio Kaigetsu died the year the war ended. Good people and bad, they all are gone.

❦

When Kaigetsu died there was a query from the Tanio family on the matter of the dissection, and it would seem therefore that Kaigetsu still meant to honor his promise of thirty years before. The times being what they were, however, there was little I could do. I finally had to let the contract I had made with Kaigetsu in Leyden come to nothing.

It is drawing on toward evening, and the wind from the lake is chilly. It is especially chilly at the collar and knees. Here it is May, and I feel as if I should be wearing wool The roaring in my ears is especially strong today. Exactly as if the wind were blowing. And indeed the wind has grown stronger.

I suppose the house will be in a turmoil by now. It will be good for them all. It will bring them to their senses. Maybe Yokoya and Sugiyama at the university have been told of the crisis, and the two of them have come running to hear the worst about their old benefactor, their faces suggesting suitable concern. They cut a considerable swathe as professors at the university, but have they inherited in the slightest degree my qualities as a scholar? They seem to have no real understanding for my work. "Professor Miike, Professor Miike," they say with great shows of respect when I am around. You would think they could find better things to do. No doubt it is "old fogey, old fogey" when I am out of sight—I feel quite certain it is. I remember well enough how those two were during the war. "Let's get the university out in the country, let's get the students organized for the war effort." Off they went and forgot all about their studies. I didn't say anything then, but I saw their limitations as scholars, and I was very sad. Whatever they are, they cannot be called scholars.

Little waves are breaking around the rickety pier where Atsuko rented her boat. There are ripples all over the lake, I see now. The white flags waving from the masts have probably been forgotten. Someone should have taken them in. I have found it more and more annoying these last years to see things that should be put away and are not. Everything has to be where it belongs. In the old days I was not so fussy. The people in the house have made me what I am. Unless I speak to her time after time, Haruko does nothing about the laundry I see from my study, and Hiroyuki leaves stamped and addressed letters lying on his desk for days on end. Kyōko and Sadamitsu too are partly to blame. And it is not only the family. The people at the university are as bad. A year has gone by since I asked for a short report on the lymph gland, and it was the youngest research student of them all who finally came around with an interim report.

I don't want to think about anything. To think is to exhaust yourself. I don't want to think about anything except *The Arterial System of the Japanese*. I have wasted a day on trivialities, and I must work tonight. Work, work, Miike Shuntarō, old scholar, must go on with his work while he lives. Tonight I must write explanations for the illustrations to Part Nine, or if not the full explanations at least the headings. Yes, and I must ask the maid to bring saké so that I can have a drink when I've finished work and am ready for bed. Two hundred grams of good saké, in a carefully washed decanter. Work that I could once have finished in an hour now takes a day, sometimes even two days or three. Growing old is a terrible thing.

Fifty years ago when I was in this room I thought only of dying. Youth has no sense of values. Today I want to live even one day more. Professor Schalbe is dead, and Professor Yamaoka of Tokyo is dead. I am sure that neither was ready to die. Both must have wanted to live and work even a day longer. Tanio Kaigetsu too. It was his great ambition to compile a Sanskrit dictionary, but he does not seem to have lived to finish it. Priests and ministers I suppose have their own special views on life and death—but Kaigetsu was not a priest. He was a scholar. It was precisely because he was a scholar among scholars that I so liked and admired him. I don't think Kaigetsu was ready to die. Enlightenment, they call it, but I suspect that enlightenment is in the last analysis a convenient refuge for the lazy. Man was meant to work furiously to the end. Why else was he created? Not to bask in the sun, surely. Not just to be happy.

I wanted to see Hira today. I wanted to see Hira so much that I could not help myself. I sent Haruko from the room and tried to control my annoyance. I made myself a bowl of tea, but the rancor was still there. As I drank from that Hagi bowl and set it on my knee, the image of Hira floated before me. By the time the man from the Ōmoriya was ringing the doorbell my mind was made up. Hira was calling me with a strength I could not resist. I have been sitting here half a day now, and I have looked at Hira enough. The face of Hira, so deep and rich in the daylight, has these last few minutes grown pale, and the sky outlining it has become almost too bright. Another hour and Hira will have melted back into the darkness.

The azaleas were beautiful today as we came past Keagé. Possibly, since they belong to the same family, the rhododendrons are in bloom at the summit of Hira. Somewhere high on that slope, the white flowers are blooming. The great white clusters spread over the face of the mountain. Ah, how much more at peace I would be if I could lie there at the summit under those scented clusters! To lie with my legs stretched out and to look up into the night sky—I am happier even at the thought of it. There and only there, I somehow feel, is what could rock me and lull me, give me peace. I should have gone up there, at least once. It is too late now. It is no longer possible for me to climb mountains. I have less chance of climbing Hira than of finishing *The Arterial System of the Japanese*.

On the snowy day when I came here in a cotton priest's robe, and at the time of the Keisuké affair, and when I went rowing with Atsuko, I saw Hira. My eye was on Hira. But I did not have the slightest desire to climb it. Why? Because the season was wrong? No, not that. Perhaps until now I have not had the qualifications. That is the point, I am sure of it.

Long ago, as I looked at the picture of the rhododendrons of Hira, I thought that the day must come when I would climb to the top. Perhaps the day was today. But today, however much I may want to, I cannot climb Hira.

Well, back into the room. I must hurry through dinner and get on with my work. How many years has it been since I last had a quiet evening away from the voices of the children? A bell is ringing somewhere. Or is an old man's ear imagining things? But I do hear a bell, behind the roaring in my ears. No, it is my imagination. I was working in a German mountain lodge (I had gone there to prepare a paper for a discussion with Dr. Steda of the red bones he had found in Siberia), and I heard the cowbells ringing. What a lovely sound it was. Perhaps something has made me hear it again, in my memory, from those tens of years ago.

Hurry with dinner, please. I have work to do. I must go back into the world of red veins, into the coral grove.

Passage to Fudaraku

Translated by
James T. Araki

Not until the spring of 1565, the year in which he must himself put out to sea, did Konkō, Abbot of the Fudaraku-ji, meditate earnestly on the Buddhists who had set sail for the island of Fudaraku. True, he had occasionally thought of his predecessors whose sailings he had witnessed, but his musings now were pervaded with an unusual sense of urgency.

Konkō had in fact never before given serious thought to the possibility of his embarking on such a voyage. His immediate predecessor as abbot had left these shores of Hama-no-miya in 1560, when he was sixty-one-years old, and the two abbots before him had done so when they were sixty-one, in November of 1545 and November of 1541. Although the three had set sail from Hama-no-miya on the south Kumano coast in November of their sixty-first year, with the Pure Land known as Fudaraku as their destination, there was no rule requiring the abbot of the monastery to do so.

The Fudaraku-ji, as its name suggests, was the fountainhead of the worship of Fudaraku. The monastery had long been known as a counterpart of Fudaraku Island—a realm in the southern region, the Pure Land of the deity of mercy, Kannon—and it had become a custom for devout worshipers to set sail from the Kumano coast for the mythical isle in the hope of being received by Kannon incarnate, in whose Pure

Land they would be reborn. Hama-no-miya in time became the customary site for departure, and the Fudaraku-ji the monastery responsible for overseeing the ritual sailing. Persons bound for the mythical isle customarily took lodging at this monastery because of its deep-rooted associations with the belief in Fudaraku. Moreover, several former abbots of the monastery were included among the nine revered as sages for having sailed to Fudaraku—the youngest, according to records kept at the monastery, at the age of eighteen, and the eldest at the age of eighty.

Because the three who had preceded Konkō as abbot had put out to sea when they were sixty-one, people came to assume that every abbot of the Fudaraku-ji would embark upon a like voyage in November of his sixty-first year. The tradition associated with the monastery served rather naturally to reinforce the assumption, and Konkō, now sixty-one, would have to submit to the dictates of popular expectation. That he had not fully understood the necessity was doubtless due to his innocence of worldly affairs, for he had known only the clergy since his youth.

Konkō had at times reflected on the meaning of his role as abbot of the Fudaraku-ji, on the possibility of his presently feeling compelled to attempt the voyage; he regarded the prospect not wholly without anticipation. He was aware of a vague, self-imposed obligation. Dedicated to serving the Buddha, he regarded the eventual voyage with some fascination, yearning perhaps. He still recalled very vividly the dignity of Shōkei at the time of his departure, and had long wished he might some day emulate this monk, who had been his teacher. Shōkei had attained enlightenment when he was sixty-one, but Konkō, aware of his own inadequacies, had never believed he could go so far without devoting himself to spiritual austerities over a long period of time— surely many more years than had been required of his teacher. He had been immersed in the traditions of the Fudaraku-ji for the better part of his life, and he longed desperately for a spiritual insight that would inspire him to embark upon the voyage.

The year 1565 was to be an unexpectedly baneful one for Konkō. No sooner did the new year dawn than visitors began to ask him "When in November do you mean to sail?" or, solicitously, "Now that the long-awaited year has come, won't you tell me how I might be of assistance?"—questions they earlier would have considered indelicate. Now, however, all visitors seemed to feel obliged to touch on this matter— as if not to do so would be a discourtesy—and well-meant concern was reflected on their faces and in their voices as well.

No one would have addressed the abbot with malice. Since his youth Konkō had disciplined himself severely. He had not achieved any great distinction, but he had an unassuming, pleasing manner. And in due course, after he was past his middle age, he came to be accorded a remarkable degree of trust and respect by the faithful. Over the past few years he had not once failed to notice the suggestion of reverence and affection in the eyes of whomever he chanced to meet— villager, Buddhist parishioner, even the ascetic Shinto priests of Nachi Falls. There was no questioning the respect and fondness he now inspired in everyone who knew him.

Konkō was disconcerted by the growing expectations. He hoped to dispel them at an early opportunity: he would have it understood that his sailing would not take place until some future year when he was spiritually prepared for it, and that a voyage to Fudaraku undertaken without conviction or faith would likely be a failure. By spring, however, he came to despair of making his intentions known. Had there been only a few to convince, he might have prevailed. But he had to contend not with a mere dozen or even one or two hundred people, but the collective expectations of the whole region.

Whenever Konkō ventured out from the monastery he would be showered with coins—offerings to His Reverence.

Children, too, ran after him and threw coins. Beggars began to follow him through the streets to pick up the offerings for themselves. The monastery began receiving cenotaphs, customarily kept in homes, together with requests that they be taken by Konkō and delivered to the Pure Land of Kannon. There were some who went so far as to entrust him with cenotaphs made for themselves.

In these circumstances Konkō seemed to have little choice. Had he mentioned his reluctance to set sail or suggested a postponement until some future year, his words would have fallen on unsympathetic ears, and he might have provoked great disquiet and even violence.

The personal disgrace would not have mattered to Konkō, but he could not have endured doing injury to the religion of Kannon. Insignificant though he might be, he was a member of the clergy. If by word or action he were to do injury to the faith, he could not possibly expect divine forgiveness even in death.

On the day of the vernal equinox, Konkō announced formally that he would put out to sea in November. The announcement was accompanied by ancient rites at the Kumano Shrine. Having been a participant on seven previous occasions, he was best acquainted with the proceedings and gave instructions on the proper order of events, as well as all the details of the floral offerings and ritual music. Whatever he recited from memory was recorded dutifully by his disciple, a seventeen-year-old monk named Seigen.

At the sight of the youth, Konkō thought of himself at twenty-seven, seated beside Yūshin, then preparing to make his departure, and noting down Yūshin's instructions. If Seigen was to remain at the Fudaraku-ji, then he, too, several decades hence must embark for Fudaraku. The young monk with freshly shaven head, Konkō thought, was as pitiful as himself.

⚜

The date of the first sailing for Fudaraku is not known. The old chronicles which Konkō consulted state that the first to embark was Keiryō, who left the Kumano coast on November 3 in the eleventh year of the Jōgan Era, some six centuries before the Eiroku Era of Konkō's time. The second was Ushin, who set sail fifty years later, in February of 919. A brief note suggests that he most likely was a monk who had left the far north in the hope of embarking upon the voyage, and had sojourned for some months or years at the Fudaraku-ji prior to his departure. The third was Kōgan, in November of 1130, following an interval of more than two hundred years. Some three centuries later, in November of 1443, Yūson became the fourth to set sail for Fudaraku. In November of 1498, seven years before Konkō was born, Seiyū put out to sea. Seiyū's exemplary erudition and virtuous attainments were yet well remembered when Konkō first came to the Fudaraku-ji. A thirty-three year interval preceded the next sailing, of Yūshin, whom Konkō had known well—a monk with eccentric ways, better remembered as the blessed Ashida, a sobriquet he acquired because he habitually wore *ashida*, the common wooden clogs, instead of the sandals appropriate to his vocation.

The belief was commonly held that the Fudaraku-ji existed as a convenience for voyagers to the isle of Fudaraku; and that since early times all Buddhists with good sense had come there, had the appropriate rites conducted, and promptly put out to sea. But Konkō knew well that such was not the case. Excluding the first four voyagers and the former abbots of Fudaraku-ji mentioned in early documents, only two or three among the many believed to have made the voyage seemed actually to have set sail. Notices of voyages undertaken by a warrior named Shimokōbe Yukihidé in 1233 and the priestly courtier Gidō in 1475 appear also in records of other monasteries, and so these doubtless were authentic cases. As for the others, there was little or no evidence.

Though sailings for Fudaraku had come to be accepted as commonplace, over a period of six hundred years no more than nine or ten persons had actually put out to sea. And this was only reasonable. Rarely would a man become prepared spiritually to covet dying at sea as the culmination of his faith. The ones who did were most uncommon monks, a scattering among thousands or myriads, unlikely to appear any oftener than once in decades, even hundreds of years.

There had all the same been an unaccountable increase in the number of voyagers; including Seishin, who had departed five years before, in all seven had left these shores during the sixty years of Konkō's lifetime. Among the seven were two young men of twenty-one and eighteen. The zeal for discarding life in the hope of being reborn in the Pure Land was itself the ultimate consummation—this was the essential teaching of the writ, in all its countless scrolls.

Never before, until the beginning of the stir in 1565, had Konkō doubted the meaning of the ritual voyage. The voyager would be confined in a doorless wooden box nailed securely to the bottom of a boat; his only provisions would be an oil lamp that would burn out in a matter of days and a small quantity of food. To be cast off thus from the Kumano coast meant certain death at sea. The instant the voyager drew his last breath, the boat would begin carrying his body speedily southward, like a bamboo leaf skimming rapids, toward the isle of Fudaraku. There he would acquire new life, that he might live eternally in the service of Kannon.

A sailing from the shores of Kumano held the promise of an end to mortal life and the beginning of spiritual life. Not doubting this, Konkō had noticed in the faces of past voyagers only the unusual serenity and composure that radiate from the hearts of those who have attained to absolute faith. He had seen joy in anticipation of new life, never sadness or fear. The voyagers had seemed tranquil and yet jubilant, and the onlookers, though understandably curious, had seemed wholly intent on glorifying them.

After he had announced his departure, Konkō began to think differently of voyagers of the past. Waking and sleeping, he saw the several he had known, their faces somehow different.

Konkō secluded himself in his cell through the spring and summer. Should he have stepped outside the monastery, people would have continued to throw coins his way, bow and pray to him as if he were a Buddha, and ask him, among other things, to take this or that to the Pure Land or lay his healing hand on the forehead of a dying man. This was so much bother for Konkō, who was now preoccupied with somehow cultivating a genuine willingness to sail for Fudaraku when the time came, three or four months hence. Faced rather suddenly with the inevitability of putting out to sea, he was forced to acknowledge the utter inadequacy of his spiritual preparations. Now he spent his waking hours reciting the scriptures. Whenever an attendant went to his room, there he would be, facing a wall, reading from the scriptures.

Occasionally he would stop, and he would be staring blankly at some object in his room; seldom did he turn to face the attendant, who, when asked, had this same ready description: "They say that the saints are *yorori* the minute they put out to sea, but His Reverence already looks every inch a *yorori*."

There was indeed a saying that a saint at sea becomes the fish called the *yorori*. *Yorori* dwell only in the coastal waters between Cape Miki and the Cape of Shio. Fishermen of the region always release *yorori* caught in their nets; they never eat them.

Konkō was tall and thin, as the *yorori* is long and slender. But it was not the physical resemblance that prompted the comparison. It was Konkō's eyes, small and remote, dull and vacant, as if benumbed, the eyes of the *yorori*.

Konkō spent his time either in recitation, his eyes closed,

or in silence, staring blankly and vacantly. When his eyes resembled those of the *yorori*, he was thinking about one or another of the past voyagers. A few times in the course of a day, his eyes would regain, if briefly, their normal luster—moments when he suddenly became aware that he had been musing upon some voyager—and he would tell himself that he must not reminisce, that he must dispel whatever notion he had been dwelling upon, that he must instead be reciting the sutras, that all would end well if he continued to recite the sutras. And he would resume his reciting as if possessed.

No sooner had Konkō finished another recitation, however, than his eyes were lifeless—a sign that in thought he was again dwelling upon some voyager of the past. He turned to pious recitation in order to keep his eyes from becoming those of a *yorori*, to banish from his vision the faces of past voyagers which appeared and reappeared. He devoted himself to this one purpose, and the effort took its toll of him.

The first time Konkō witnessed a sailing for Fudaraku was on the occasion of the departure of Yūshin, who was forty-three years old at the time. Konkō, who only a half year earlier had moved to the monastery from a temple in his native village of Tanabé, was then twenty-seven. Yūshin had been regarded as something of an oddity because of eccentric behavior—his insistence on wearing *ashida* instead of sandals, for instance. Suddenly he seemed to become a man possessed and, to everyone's surprise, declared that he would set sail for Fudaraku. And he embarked on the voyage three months later. Because his sailing was the first in thirty-three years, it attracted considerable notice. On the appointed day, the beach at Hama-no-miya was thronged with people who had come from places as far distant as Isé and Tsu to witness the inspiring event.

Konkō and Yūshin were both from Tanabé, and this association led to an acquaintance between them and opportunities for Konkō to speak informally with him. Konkō recalled how he often would remark that he could see Fudaraku Island. When asked its location, Yūshin replied that on any clear day the island appeared distinctly on the horizon. Anyone, he added, who had freed himself of delusions and acquired faith in the Buddha could see it. Konkō too would see it if he gave himself up wholly to faith in Fudaraku.

"It is level and high," said Yūshin of this island, "rising on boulders that are pounded incessantly on all sides by the stormy sea. I can hear the pounding of the waves. This tableland with the sea all round it is an infinite expanse, calm, of untold beauty, covered with verdure that can never wither, abounding in springs that can never run dry. Great flocks of vermilion birds, their tails long and flowing, make their nests there. And I see people disporting themselves there—these people do not age as they serve the Buddha."

Yūshin completed the customary ritual and boarded his boat near the first of several sacred gates in a line from the shore. He was oblivious to the presence of well-wishers who crowded the beach, and he spoke only to Konkō, who attended him up to the moment of boarding. "Fudaraku is exceptionally clear today," Yūshin said to him. "You must join me there someday." And he laughed softly. Konkō, though he did not know why, was startled at Yūshin's smile. Yūshin's eyes, ever steady in their gaze, were suddenly piercing, and covered over by a kind of iridescence.

Yūshin's boat was escorted as far as Tsunakiri Island, some seven miles from shore, by men on several vessels and there was sent off on its solitary voyage to distant waters.

Those who had escorted Yūshin saw the boat moving directly south through the dark waves, speeding away as if it were being pulled in on a line. Perhaps the Buddha was leading it to the island that had dwelt so constantly in his vision. Monks at the Fudaraku-ji who earlier had treated him as an eccentric spoke ill of him no more. The curious actions of the monk who had worn *ashida* were seen in a new light, and each became an episode to be recounted as a legacy of his high attainment.

Konkō had been urged by Yūshin to make the same voyage one day, and now, thirty-four years later, he was about to sail for Fudaraku. Whenever Konkō thought of Yūshin, he remembered the strange greenish iridescence in his eyes. There was no doubting Yūshin's having seen the Pure Land. Were his eyes, as he studied the isle on the horizon, no different from the eyes of others? His voyage did not carry with it any promise of death. Quite probably he never thought about death. As he had failed to contemplate death, so had he failed to contemplate the renewal of life—these were not his concerns. His strangely glowing eyes had actually envisioned Fudaraku. The island became an obsession with him, and he simply decided to go there.

The sailing of Shōkei took place ten years later. When Shōkei first announced his intention to put out to sea, no one thought it remarkable. Had he lived his lifetime at the monastery, never associating himself with the belief in Fudaraku, he would have been revered no less. His decision, once it became known, was regarded by all as quite in accord with his character. This response attested to the great admiration with which people regarded this diminutive monk—so small that a child might easily pick him up—face wrinkled ten years beyond his age, eyes brimming with compassion.

Konkō was filled with sadness when he learned of Shōkei's decision, but only because he hated to say goodbye. When he remembered that he would not again hear those kind words of encouragement, those thoughtful and deeply felt admonitions, the sorrow became torment. Not even separation from the parents who had brought him into this world, he thought, could be sadder.

All through summer of that year, on now-forgotten occasions when Konkō had gone to him, Shōkei would say: "Meeting death on the blue expanse of the sea might be rather pleasant."

"Will you die?" Konkō asked, for he had never before associated these sailings with death at sea. There would be death, to be sure, but was not the purpose of it all to acquire eternal life at the end of the voyage?

"Of course I shall die," Shōkei replied. "I shall die at sea and sink to the bottom, which, by the way, is every bit as expansive as the surface, and I shall make friends with all the fishes." And he laughed merrily as if the thought gave him considerable pleasure.

When he boarded his vessel and when he sailed away from Tsunakiri Island—at all times, indeed—Shōkei was smiling as always. Earlier voyagers had had themselves shut in a box which was then fastened to the bottom of the boat. A similar box-like compartment was placed on his boat, but he did not go inside. He sat at the stern and the onlookers saw him waving goodbye. He shed no tears, but everyone else, young and old, was weeping.

Shōkei envisioned drowning at sea, not passage to Fudaraku. Why, then, did he set out on a voyage to the mythical isle?

Konkō could think of only one reason. Shōkei must have believed that he would serve Kannon best by doing so. In the decade preceding his voyage, Kumano was beset with a succession of disasters—a great earthquake in January of 1538, a landslide in August of that year and, coinciding with it, the inexplicable splintering of every rafter in the main Kumano Shrine, the typhoon of August, 1540, which swept down to the sea every river boat of the commercial guilds and caused countless deaths all along the sea coast, and a destructive flood in August of 1541. To make matters worse, the civil war raging about the capital bred violence in outlying districts. At night the region was the province of brigands, and brutality and killing were the most common of occurrences. Religion was as good as forgotten to Shōkei's unhappiness. He must be an inspiration and bring people back to religion.

Konkō was disturbed by the thought that a monk as wise

as Shōkei believed in nothing about the voyage to Fudaraku save only dying at sea. That was not enough for him. The eventuality of reaching Fudaraku Island might not have been of concern to one such as Shōkei, who had attained enlightenment. Konkō knew, however, that he could not be content with a voyage that carried no promise other than that of sinking to the floor of the sea.

Nichiyo put out to sea four years after Shōkei, whom he had succeeded as abbot of the Fudaraku-ji. Nichiyo, sickly and short-tempered, was a contrast to his predecessor. Konkō felt as though he had not had a moment's rest during the four years of his service to Nichiyo, who was feared by everyone in the monastery. When he announced his intention to set sail for Fudaraku—it was wholly unexpected—Konkō was not alone in breathing a sigh of relief. Life was very precious to Nichiyo; he would have the monastery in an uproar if he so much as caught a cold. In January of his final year his asthma was worse. Because medical treatment had no effect whatever, he concluded that he had not much longer to live. Already sixty-one, he no doubt decided that a voyage to Fudaraku was preferable to dying in a sickbed.

Surely Nichiyo was influenced very strongly by the hope of reaching the Pure Land alive. Since autumn of the year before, he had talked more frequently, and to anyone who would listen, about extraordinary accounts in books he had read—typically, about a monk from such and such province having set sail from Tosa in January of 1142 and having lived to reach Fudaraku Island and to return to Japan with a knowledge of the Pure Land. In arriving at his decision Nichiyo was encouraged immeasurably by these confused accounts. Nevertheless from the time he made the decision until the scheduled day of departure his deportment was consistent with his exalted role. He seemed to acquire unusual confidence at the time the title of sage was conferred upon him and throughout the summer and autumn months he was serene. To all appearances he had no doubts about life and death.

On the day before his departure, Nichiyo walked down to the shore to inspect his boat. He seemed displeased and asked Konkō, who was with him, "Did Shōkei ride out in a boat as small as this?" Konkō replied that it had been an even smaller one.

The next day as Nichiyo was boarding the boat one foot slid into the water. He seemed very unhappy, indeed wretched. His expression was one of such despair as Konkō had not known before. He stood motionless for a time, his dry foot on the boat and his wet foot on the gangplank, and then stepped aboard as if resigning himself to fate. The five who had accompanied him as far as Tsunakiri Island said later that he spoke not one word to them.

Though twenty years had passed, Konkō could still see Nichiyo's expression clearly. It reflected, though he did not like to think so, his own feelings of the moment.

Bankei, who embarked upon the voyage when he was forty-two, had like Yūshin often remarked that he could see Fudaraku Island. He was a tall, stout man, with a somewhat unruly disposition. Though Konkō had never liked him, he was strangely moved when Bankei, ten years younger than he, announced that he would embark for Fudaraku. Bankei was a giant compared to the frail, diminutive voyagers of the past—much too large, it seemed, to be accommodated by the customary boat. His was not the image one could readily associate with the ritual voyage.

Bankei believed that he would live to see Fudaraku Island. "I don't want to die," he often said. "I'll get to the island safely because it beckons me. I can actually see it, and that most certainly means it beckons me there." He was inclined to ramble on in this vein.

No one gave Bankei the reassurance he sought—with the

single exception of Nichiyo's successor, the abbot Seishin, who invariably responded with kind and reassuring words.

Seishin also embarked for Fudaraku when he was sixty-one, and, Konkō knew, for a reason distinctly different from the other voyagers. Seishin, who had no kin, was a lonely man. During the time he was abbot he was victim of a series of unhappy deceptions and betrayals. His feelings, like his frail body, were easily injured. He became hopelessly misanthropic, weary of society and of people and life.

Konkō and Seishin got along well with each other, perhaps because they were so near the same age. The weariness that possessed Seishin in his old age was complete, and he longed for death above all else. He was not a man of firm religious conviction even though he had been a member of the order since his youth. He veiled his true thoughts, of course, and managed to complete the customary rites and earn the respect and reverence due a monk embarking upon the ritual voyage. Only Konkō knew how he really felt.

Not long before the appointed day Seishin said that he would rather walk into the sea striking a bell, and continue walking until he sank beneath the deep waters; but he was dissuaded by his disciples. He departed with dignity as Shōkei had.

"I want to reach Fudaraku as quickly as possible," he said. "Therefore I need no food or fuel. All I need is a boat with a mast and a sail that bears the inscription 'Praise to the Lord Amida.'" That was precisely as he had it.

Seishin carried a rosary, but in other respects he bore few of the marks of a Buddhist. He did not intone prayers or finger his beads as his predecessors had.

"At last," he said, as his boat was being cast off from Tsunakiri Island. "A man is a trial to others whether he's trying to live or die. But I suppose it must be so." He seemed happy to be finally alone, free of the many well-wishers.

There were yet two other voyagers: twenty-one-year-old Kōrin and eighteen-year-old Zenkō, who put out to sea when

Konkō was in his thirties, the former in 1530 and the latter in 1533. The youths were sick and to all appearances on the verge of death when they came to the monastery, accompanied by their parents, to request passage to Fudaraku. Kōrin had been urged to do so by his parents, who believed that he might by some miracle live to see the island paradise. He apparently knew little about the ritual voyage. He knew, however, that his illness was mortal, and had chosen to abide by his parents' wishes. Zenkō was carrying out his own wish. His parents had wanted him to live on and he sought to persuade them that he would die at sea and be carried by the currents to the Pure Land of Fudaraku; they were sadly troubled when they brought him to the monastery.

The youths were accompanied to Tsunakiri Island by large groups of well-wishers, and on both occasions the beach was crowded. Konkō had been moved to tears at the sight of the emaciated Zenkō putting out to sea, and at the recollection all the sorrow returned.

✿

Summer was speeding by. Konkō each day would ask someone to tell him what day of the month it was, and each time doubt his ears. He continued to spend his waking hours reciting from the scriptures. After the autumnal equinox the days passed with astonishing speed. The light of dawn seemed instantly to fade into dusk.

Konkō knew well that he was no better prepared spiritually than before. The faces of past voyagers continued to appear and reappear. However fondly he might regard them, they now seemed unrelated to Fudaraku. The grandeur that had fascinated him was gone.

The faces of Yūshin and Bankei—both had often said they could see Fudaraku Island—now seemed somehow aberrant. The voyage of Seishin, obviously undertaken in desperation by a thoroughly weary old man, could have had nothing to do with belief in Kannon or the Pure Land. He had only watched the dark waves running in turbulent succession upon the Kumano coast. In this respect he was no different from Konkō's teacher, Shōkei, who had displayed such remarkable dignity on his departure. Shōkei had been certain of imminent death and had noticed only the surging sea on which his mortal remains would rest. He must not have been concerned with reaching Fudaraku and acquiring new life. His serene eyes were those of one who left such concerns behind.

Nichiyo was a man with a set purpose. At his departure, as he sailed, and days or even weeks later with no more than a plank to keep him afloat, perhaps he clung to life, still hoping to be rescued, to have Kannon reach out for him. He hoped for a miracle. He had, in the deepest sense, had no part of faith or of belief in Kannon or Fudaraku. He had seemed to believe, but had not believed.

Though both Kōrin and Zenkō had moved the onlookers profoundly with an appearance of serenity, their voyages had in fact had nothing whatsoever to do with faith. Wasted from illness, they were able to resign themselves to death with less hesitation than most others.

When Konkō became aware that he had been gazing at their several faces, he would hastily dismiss them. They were utterly dreary. He would not wish to resemble them, and yet he felt that his face would be any one of theirs the moment he slackened his hold upon himself.

If he was to embark on the voyage, Konkō thought, he would not want to look like any of his predecessors. What would his expression be then? He did not quite know, but it must be one that would be appropriate to a truly devout monk setting sail for Fudaraku. If he must put out to sea, he would do so wearing an expression appropriate to his role.

In October, with the date of sailing just one month away, Konkō began to think differently of the faces of past voyagers. He underwent another change. He would give anything to be like one of them—it did not matter which one. He had felt as if he could at will resemble any one of the faces, even though the thought was repugnant to him. Now that he longed to be like them, however, he knew that he had been indulging in wishfulness. He had set himself a hard task.

If only he might see the Pure Land! He recalled with envy the extraordinary glow in the eyes of Yūshin and Bankei. He envied Seishin's expression of complete relief on gaining the solitude he had long sought. He regarded enviously even Nichiyo's expression, usually sullen as if to reflect some inner turmoil but capable of anger when he was disturbed, as when his foot slid into the water. There was little likelihood of attaining the calmness and dignity of Shōkei. Konkō even doubted that he could resemble either of the two youths. How were they able at such a tender age to assume expressions of such utter tranquillity and resignation?

Kenkō received callers, who were suddenly numerous. He did not know who they were or why they had come. He had neither the will nor the ability to remember. In the morning an attendant would lead him to the Thousand-armed Kannon in the main hall, and there he would sit until noon. Callers would come one after another into the hall. Konkō did not speak to them. Having come to say goodbye, they seemed relieved that he did not. They seemed to conclude that in these circumstances words were an inappropriate means of farewell, and Konkō's silence seemed not at all strange.

If a visitor spoke to him, Konkō did not answer. He recited a holy text softly or sat in silence, his eyes like those of a *yorori*, fixed vacantly upon a darkened corner of the hall.

By November he had lost all awareness of time. When he awoke he would call Seigen. "Isn't this the day for my voyage?" he would ask. Told that it was not, he would lift his head in apparent relief, and look upon the white sands of the garden. He would gaze at the bright green plantings and listen to the lapping of waves on the beach of Hama-no-miya, which was like an extension of the garden. Only recently had he begun to notice trees and the sound of waves. He perceived things which he had not in many years.

On one of those bright, clear autumn days, Konkō asked again if it was not the day for his voyage.

"You will be leaving this afternoon at four," Seigen replied. Konkō stood up and sat down again. His strength seemed to have been drained quite away. He was perfectly still, quite incapable of motion.

An attendant came to say that a group of well-wishing Shinto priests had come from Nachi Falls. Another announced the arrival of a Zen abbot.

Konkō at last seemed aware of the stir. With the assistance of several attendants he changed clothes. With several monks in the lead he went to the main hall, where he had sat in meditation every morning since first coming to the monastery. He glanced calmly at the Thousand-armed Kannon, Taishaku, Bonten, and other deities. Soon he was staring at them intently.

Every activity was now dictated by his attendants. He sat before the central image and recited from the scriptures, then returned to his assigned position and sat, gazing intently at the images. The air was thick with incense. The assemblage of monks flowed out of the small hall over the corridors to the garden. The hall itself seemed enfolded in the fullness of the chorus of prayer.

Shortly past noon, Konkō retired from the main hall to the cloister, where he had tea with several monks. A sack containing one hundred and eight pebbles, each inscribed with one word from the scriptures, was brought to the veranda. Several sacred scrolls, a statuette of the Buddha, clothing, and a few other items—all to be placed in Konkō's boat—were also gathered on the veranda and inspected by the attendants. And, finally, a wooden palanquin to carry these items was brought in and deposited in a manner which one might have thought unnecessarily casual. Though somewhat annoyed by the rough casualness, he did not feel inclined to protest.

The monks left the monastery shortly before the appointed hour. Unseasonably brilliant sunlight filled Konkō's eyes. The strand was thronged with people. The party of monks, Konkō at its center, moved along with the excited crowd, passed through the sacred gate, and came to the white sand along the shore.

As had Nichiyo years before him, Konkō thought that his boat was the smallest of them all. He wondered why they had given him such a tiny boat. There was no boat landing. His boat and three others for those who would see him off lay at the water's edge, as if they had been washed ashore. The three were much larger than Konkō's.

He was led aboard his boat at once. Workmen came aboard with a large wooden box which they placed over him. He was suddenly angry. The boat should have had a compartment which he could enter. Instead one had been brought afterwards.

There was a pounding as it was nailed to the boat. Presently the pounding stopped. It was dark inside the box. A door was opened, and various articles were pushed inside. Konkō was asked to come out of the box and greet the onlookers, and he did so. The crowd stirred. Coins fell like rain on to the boat and along the shoreline and children fought to collect them. Konkō fled back inside. He sat for some time in the dark while a mast and a sail bearing the formula "Praise to the Lord Amida" were put up. Everything seemed clumsy and slow.

Almost two hours passed. With not a word of warning to him, the boat began to move. He felt it grinding against the pebble-strewn shore, and then there was the smoothness of the sea. He wanted to look out, but he could not open the box. It had been tightly sealed. However hard he pushed, he could not loosen a single one of the boards.

Then he heard the sound of an oar. He was not alone, then. The boatman would steer the vessel as far as Tsunakiri Island. There he would be cast off, alone.

He began to hear an intermittent chiming of bells through

the sound of waves. Straining his ears, he heard a chanting of sacred words to the accompaniment of the chimes. But the chanting would be interrupted by the waves. Though at times it would assume a festive gaiety, it was soon obliterated by the roar of the sea.

As the boats made land at Tsunakiri Island, Konkō found a slit and pressed his face to it. Night was approaching and the dark billowing sea seemed infinite.

"It's goodbye, Your Reverence!" the boatman called from above. Konkō was confused. It was customary for voyagers to spend the night on Tsunakiri Island with the rest of the party and set sail in the morning.

"I'm to stay here tonight!" Konkō shouted, so loudly in fact that he was surprised by his own voice.

"We're sending you off right now instead of waiting until tomorrow," the boatman answered. "The weather is bad, and we don't want to be stranded here."

Konkō again cried out, but there was no answer. The boatman had already leapt ashore.

The boat was now pitching and rolling. Konkō saw that the sea was much darker now, a broad expanse of turbulence.

At last he was alone. He sank to the floor. He felt the full weariness of the day and drifted helplessly into sleep.

Some hours later he awoke. In pitch darkness, he felt the boards beneath him rising and falling. He heard the crashing of waves below him, then overhead.

He quickly raised himself and with all his might threw himself against the side of the box. Never before had he resorted to such violence.

He repeated it in desperation five and six times. A board flew loose, and into the compartment came a blast of wind and spray. The box catching the wind sent the boat into a lurch. The next instant Konkō felt himself being flung into the sea.

⚓

He clung to a plank and stayed afloat through the night. At daybreak he saw Tsunakiri Island close at hand. As a child he had swum often in the coastal waters, and so he was able to save himself.

Around noon he was washed ashore, plank and all. He lay there until evening, when he was noticed by one of the monks who had accompanied him to the island the day before. The party of well-wishers had been detained there because of the high seas.

Konkō was given a meal there on the bleak shore. The monks, meanwhile, were huddled together discussing at length what to do. They asked a fisherman for a boat and put Konkō in it. Konkō by then had regained some of his strength. "Spare me," he said, in a barely audible voice. Some of the monks must have heard him, but no one seemed to understand.

The boat was left on the beach for a while, and several men stood around it, regarding it in silence.

The young monk Seigen saw his teacher's lips apparently forming words, though surely not from the scriptures. He leaned close, but he heard nothing. He took out paper and brush and ink. With trembling hand, Konkō strung together these words:

> Of mythical isles, of Hōrai,
> I have known two and ten.
> Believe only in the Pure Land.
> I shall believe in Lord Amida.

The words were barely legible. Again Konkō wrote:

> Should you seek Kannon,
> Believe not in Fudaraku.
> Should you seek Fudaraku,
> Believe not in the sea.

Konkō put down the brush and immediately closed his eyes. Seigen wondered if his teacher was dead, but he detected a pulse. He studied the words. Their meaning escaped him. They might perhaps be evidence of enlightenment and again they might indicate anger and frustration, no more.

A hastily made box was lowered over Konkō and attached securely to the bottom of the boat. Then Konkō and the boat were pushed out to sea.

🙟

Thereafter the abbots of the Fudaraku-ji were no longer expected to put out to sea when they reached sixty-one. There had been no such rule to begin with. As the account of Konkō's voyage became known, it seems, people changed their minds about the role of the abbot of the Fudaraku-ji. Thereafter, when an abbot died, his body was sent out to sea from Hama-no-miya. The ritual voyage was called "passage to Fudaraku." There were seven such voyages over the next one hundred and fifty years. Because the sailing took place during the month in which the abbot died, it could be at any time of the year.

There was one more instance of a living embarkation for Fudaraku: Seigen's, thirteen years after Konkō's, in November of 1578. Seigen was thirty at the time and the records of the Fudaraku-ji inform us that he put out to sea for the sake of his parents. As for the thoughts of this young monk, who had accompanied Konkō to Tsunakiri Island, we have no means of knowing them.

Acts of Worship Seven Stories
Yukio Mishima/Translated by John Bester

These seven consistently interesting stories, each with its own distinctive atmosphere and mood, are a timely reminder of Mishima the consummate writer.

Sun and Steel
Yukio Mishima/Translated by John Bester

This fascinating document—part autobiography, part reflections on the search for personal identity—traces Mishima's life from an introverted childhood to a creative maturity.

House of Nire
Morio Kita/Translated by Dennis Keene

A comic novel that captures the essence of Japanese society while chronicling the lives of the Nire family and their involvement in the family-run mental hospital.

Stranger in Tibet
The Adventures of a Wandering Zen Monk
Scott Berry

The fascinating biography of a young Zen monk who managed to enter the forbidden city of Lhasa during the turn of the century.

Singular Rebellion
Saiichi Maruya/Translated by Dennis Keene

A comic novel about a man who abandons middle-aged convention for life with a young model and her grandmother, a convicted murderer.

BEST SELLING TITLES NOW AVAILABLE IN PAPERBACK

Literature

THE DOCTOR'S WIFE
Sawako Ariyoshi/Translated by Wakako Hironaka & Ann Siller Kostant
"An excellent story." —*Choice*

THE LAKE
Yasunari Kawabata/Translated by Reiko Tsukimura
By Japan's only Nobel Prize–winning author.

POINTS AND LINES
Japan's Best-Selling Mystery
Seichō Matsumoto/Translated by Makiko Yamamoto & Paul C. Blum

THE RELUCTANT ADMIRAL
Yamamoto and the Imperial Navy
Hiroyuki Agawa/Translated by John Bester

MATSUO BASHŌ
The Master Haiku Poet
Makoto Ueda

ALMOST TRANSPARENT BLUE
Ryu Murakami/Translated by Nancy Andrew
"A Japanese mix of *Clockwork Orange* and *L'Etranger*." —*Newsweek*

THE DAY MAN LOST
Hiroshima, 6 August 1945
The Pacific War Research Society

THE HAIKU HANDBOOK
How to Write, Share, and Teach Haiku
William J. Higginson with Penny Harter
Available only in Japan.